A REVERSE HAREM NOVEL

LIARS

BOOK TWO IN THE TRIAD SERIES

DANA ISALY

LIARS
Copyright © 2021 Dana Isaly
All rights reserved.
Published: Dana Isaly 2021

No parts of this book may be reproduced in any form without written consent from the author. Except in the use of brief quotations in a book review.
This book is a piece of fiction. Any names, characters, businesses, places or events are a product of the author's imagination or are used fictitiously. Any resemblance to persons living or dead, events or locations is purely coincidental.
This book is licensed for your personal enjoyment only. This book may not be resold or given away to other people. If you are reading this book and have not purchased it for your use only, then you should return it to your favorite book retailer and purchase your own copy.
Thank you for respecting the author's work.

Editing: Sandra at One Love Editing
Cover Design: Pink Elephant Designs
Formatting: Pink Elephant Designs

To the readers that made my dreams come true.

AUTHOR'S *note*

Content Warning:

This book is strictly for those over the age of legal adulthood. It is a reverse harem with dark themes such as BDSM, violence, lots of bad words, and group activities.

PREFACE

SCARLET

I laughed like a fucking madwoman. Even as they sliced at another part of me and kicked me in the mouth. I spat out blood and laughed as some dripped into my nose. God, that burned like a bitch, but I laughed even harder. The world was upside down as I hung from chains that rattled on the floor and dug into my legs.

All I could think was…

Where were my boys?

CHAPTER one

SEBASTIAN

Two Weeks Earlier

"Sebastian," Elliot said with a sigh as I continued to line each and every one of those motherfuckers up against the outside of the warehouse. She wasn't inside when we arrived, and my mind has been racing ever since. She wasn't there. We didn't get there in time. And now the assholes that I had lined up like the bad kids at recess were going to pay the price for it.

"Just let him do what he needs to do," I heard Tristan say behind me.

Too fucking right, I thought to myself.

These fucking assholes took my girl, killed Melody, killed our men, and tricked us into a false location to try and swarm us. They didn't deserve to live. They didn't even deserve a quick death. No, I wasn't going to let them die with a gunshot to the head or the heart. I was going to make them suffer for it.

I glanced over my shoulder and saw both Tristan and Elliot half-heartedly holding their guns towards the line of men. We had overcome them easily, seeing as we had the forethought to bring reinforcements with us. Most of our men that were still with us were inside doing cleanup. I looked back to the dozen or so men I had lined up against the charred outer wall of the warehouse. The fire we had set to the place before hadn't managed to destroy the entire place, so they had sought out the undamaged areas like rats. I walked down the line of them, tossing and twisting my knife in my hand. I made eye contact with all of them as I made my way past them all.

As I made it to the last man in the line, he gave me a sickly grin and then spat on my boots.

Motherfucker.

"Those were my favorite pair," I stated blandly. "I guess you wanted to go first since you decided to be the one to poke the bear?" I asked him. His long, stringy black hair was plastered to his face, and blood ran slowly down his forehead. I looked him over, and my eyes snagged on his hands. They were covered in claw marks.

My hand found his throat, and a sick sense of happiness rocketed through me when I heard his skull make contact with the stone wall behind him.

"Did you touch her?" I asked. I felt Tristan and Elliot take a few steps towards me.

"In what way?"

"Did you touch her?" I asked again, slamming him back against the wall by his throat. His eyes rolled back for a moment before he regained full consciousness.

"Oh, I touched her," he sneered. "My hands were all over that smooth, creamy skin, and I watched her flush under my touch like the needy little gypsy she is. You not fucking her regularly enough? Or is your dick just not good enough for her?" He let out a bark of a laugh and then met my eyes again. "Wait, wait. I bet it's just because she's so fucking hungry for dick she can't help but gag on any that comes near her, right?"

He didn't get a chance to say anything else because my knife found its way under his chin and up through his mouth. Blood gushed from his lips as I used my other hand to slam his head again into the wall. And again. And again. I threw his head into the stone until I felt his skull crack and blood seep over my fingers. His eyes shut, and his body went limp.

I yanked the knife out of his head and then stepped back, letting him fall to the floor in a heap. I looked up to the next man in line and grinned. I knew I could look like a terrifying bastard if I wanted to. And at that moment, I wanted to.

"He's pissed himself," Elliot said, sounding disgusted.

I laughed and walked to stand in front of the guy. He was so scared, he was shaking. Honestly, these people needed to find better men for their gang. This was pathetic. Every single one of them was shaking, pissing themselves, or had tears running down their face. I flipped my bloody knife in the air, letting it spray some blood on the guy in front of me as it twirled and then landed in my palm.

"Quit showboating and just do it already," Elliot chided from behind me.

"You're sucking the fun out of it," I answered, not taking my eyes off the guy in front of me. "They touched our girl, Elliot. Don't you think that warrants a little playtime?"

"I told him he had free rein," I heard Tristan say.

"We're wasting time. We could be using this time to try and find her." Elliot's words were like a bucket of ice water thrown over my head. He was right. I was wasting valuable time and resources by slowing down their punishment.

"Alright, I'll make this quick, then, boys. But just know that I wanted to drag this out for each and every one of you for even daring to look at Scarlet, okay?" Before I finished speaking, I had sliced through the side of pissy pants' neck. His hands went for his throat as blood sprayed and gushed through his fingers. He fell to the ground and bled out at my feet.

"Are you killing them all?

"Yes, Tristan," I said with an annoyed sigh. "Why? Do we need to keep any of them?"

"Don't you think it would be prudent to do so?" he asked. I turned around to look at him.

"Do you always have to be the voice of fucking reason?" He laughed, and I just walked up and down the line of men, waiting to see which one was going to break first. One of them was bound to be weak enough to beg for his life. None of them was smart enough to realize that even if they were spared now, they wouldn't be later on. Tristan might want one of them alive for questioning, but he wouldn't want to *keep* them alive.

"Please!" one of the men in the middle wailed. "I'll tell you whatever you want, just please, please don't kill me." The rest of the men broke down, yelling the same thing. I laughed and grabbed the one that had broken first, shoving him in the direction of Tristan. He wanted the bastard, he could babysit him.

"Calm the fuck down!" Elliot yelled to the rest of them who had started to realize their fate. They were all over the place, getting out of line and yelling at us to choose them instead.

"Too late," I said to all of them before making my way down the line and slicing the throat of each man. The further down the line I got, the less they fought me, which was kind of a disappointment. I liked it better when they fought.

"You are not getting in our clean-ass Rover dripping in blood," Tristan said as I finished the last man off, his blood soaking my already sodden shirt.

"I'll take one of the guys' motorcycles," I said as I wiped my knife on the only clean spot on my jeans.

"Alright, let's get this asshole tied up and in the boot. Then we need to go to the Westbrook house. Going back to the manor right now isn't safe. Elliot," Tristan said while pulling the guy towards the car. "Please go make sure all of the men that Seb has just butchered are actually dead. Seb," he continued as he pulled some zip ties out of the car. "Make sure the guys inside know that they need to completely destroy this place. I don't want a single fucking brick standing by the time they're done with it."

I gave a mock salute and jogged inside as I heard Elliot's gun going off in methodical shots. He would shoot all of them twice in the head, making sure they were really gone. Not that he needed to. I didn't make mistakes when it came to killing. I was a monster in men's clothing, cold and calculated. And all of those men had laid their eyes and their hands on my woman. They didn't deserve to live after that. They had paid their penance with their lives.

"Hey!" I called over to our guys, who were busy throwing petrol over the bodies and walls. "I need to take someone's bike home." I gestured to my clothes, and one of the guys, Niko, gave me a dark laugh before throwing me his keys.

"T and Elliot better give me a ride home though," he said. "I'm not riding bitch with any of these assholes."

"No worries, man," I said, catching the keys midair. "I'll let them know. We kept one of the guys alive for questioning. We're going back to the Westbrook house and will be staying there for the time being. If you guys hear anything, let us know immediately. You know the drill. And we want this entire place torched this time, nothing left standing."

"You got it, boss," Niko answered before going back

to splashing petrol along the walls. I jogged back out of the warehouse and over to the car.

"You guys need to give Niko a ride home. They'll all be out in a minute. I'll meet you at Westbrook." I looked to the boot of the Rover and felt the black wave of anger overtake me again. I didn't know what we were going to do, but we had to get her back. God knows what they were doing to her or where they had her.

"We'll get her back, Seb," Tristan assured.

"Yeah, if she wants to be found," Elliot murmured darkly.

"Excuse me?" I asked, turning my dark gaze on his.

"Elliot," Tristan warned. "Now is not the time."

"The time for what?" I shouted.

"You don't think it's weird that they found the manor? That they were able to so easily overtake everyone in that house? That they tell us a meeting place and then she isn't here?" Elliot finished, and Tristan gave a heavy sigh. I took a deep breath, trying to calm the sheer rage washing through me like a tsunami.

"What exactly are you trying to say, Elliot?"

"What if she was a plant?"

And that was the last thing Elliot said before I punched him so hard he fell to the ground, completely blacking out.

CHAPTER two

SCARLET

The Present

Everything fucking hurt. I groaned and tried to blink open my eyes but was only partly successful, seeing as blood and tears had dried and crusted my eyelids shut. The first thing I noticed was that I wasn't hanging from the ceiling anymore.

Thank god, I thought. I didn't know how long the human body could live being hung upside down like I had been, but every moment of it was torture. As they took knives to my skin, flaying my body like a fucking animal, I had alternated between screaming and laughing. I knew the screaming was exactly what they wanted. It's what got their rocks off, but I couldn't help it. At some point, the pain became too real, too all-encompassing, that I couldn't ignore it.

But the laughing? The laughing terrified them. I could see it in their eyes every time my mouth curved into a smile. They hadn't expected that, and if I was honest with myself, I hadn't either.

I rolled onto my back and whimpered in pain. I must've had multiple broken ribs to be in so much pain. Every drag of oxygen into my lungs felt like I was being kicked all over again. I blinked a few more times against the tears welling in the corners of my eyes. The added lubrication let me pry my eyes the rest of the way open.

Looking around, I tried to take in my surroundings. I definitely wasn't at the warehouse anymore. There were no windows, no tables or chairs, just white walls and a concrete floor, the last of which I was lying on. There were a few fluorescent strip lights on the ceiling that were blinking blue and orange, like the bulbs were about to blow.

Footsteps sounded from the corner of the room, where it looked like there were stairs. I stood no chance of fighting, not in my current state. Every time I made a move, my skin burned and my bones screamed. I had to fucking get out. I just had no idea how to do that after they had been torturing me for god knew how long.

"What did the boss say?" One of the voices trailed in through the door.

"We keep her here for now. They're going to give up hope and stop looking for her at some point."

"Did you not see the massacre that happened at the warehouse? They aren't going to stop looking. We're going to have to keep moving her, or they're going to find her and we'll end up like the sorry bastards at the warehouse." Each voice had a Spanish accent, and I groaned.

If they had been working for my family, I might have been able to work them over. But the drug dealers that I had a hand in killing? A good outcome was not going to be as likely.

"She's awake?" They opened the door, and I looked up at them. Their faces were obscured by bandanas from the bridge of their noses down, and they both wore hats that shaded their eyes. Both of them wore long sleeves and jeans and nondescript boots. I wouldn't be able to pick them out of a lineup with so little to look at.

"What—" I started but then began coughing violently. Each cough felt like someone was stabbing me in the sides, and I begged my body to chill the fuck out because I wasn't going to survive this amount of pain.

Once the coughing fit cleared up, I tried to wipe the tears off my face, but I couldn't even lift my arms without wanting to scream. I looked down at them and felt a whimper escape my throat. There were hundreds of cuts all over them, ranging from small little nicks to longer, angrier slashes that were still trying to seep blood. If these assholes didn't kill me, the infection from all of these cuts would. I followed the length of my body, thanking Hades himself that I still had my pajamas on. At least I wasn't naked. Life could've been worse.

The angry knife cuts extended down my legs as well, some of them much longer than the ones on my arms, and I could vaguely remember those happening. My feet were bare and dirty, covered in dried blood, but I was missing toenails on about six different toes from what I could see. I didn't remember that happening, thank fuck.

"Taking stock of your injuries, little slut?" one of the men asked.

"There are plenty more beneath the surface. Pretty sure Diego broke about three of your ribs the other day," the other one chimed in, humor filling his voice.

Fucking pricks.

"You have…no idea…what my boys…are going to…do to your sorry…asses," I ground out between ragged breaths.

"Your boys are exactly that, sweetheart," the one on the left said. "Boys. They won't find you, because we keep moving you. You get moved to a new location every few days. You just don't remember because we make sure you're knocked out cold before it happens."

"Enough," the other one said. "Stop giving her information."

"What's she going to do with it? Report back?" He snorted and placed his boot on my side, putting pressure on my bruised and broken ribs. I screamed and squeezed my eyes shut as blackness threatened my vision.

"Just fucking kill me already, then!" I shouted at them both once his boot left my side.

"That would be too easy on you though, wouldn't it?" He squatted down and got in my vision, showing me his stupid, ordinary plain brown eyes that could belong to anyone. I would never be able to tell who these people were. "After what you did, you deserve to suffer until we take you to the boss."

"That's enough, Aaron!" The one that was squatting next to me must've smiled because the skin around his eyes crinkled. He reached out and ran a finger across my lips. My stomach rolled and heaved at the thought of any of these men touching me against my will.

"She's so pretty though, Diego," Aaron said, trying to push my lips apart to get inside. I momentarily thought about letting his finger fall into my mouth just so that I could have the pleasure of biting it the fuck off. But I didn't know where it had been, and I was already in rough enough shape. If I bit him, they would probably beat me until I was near death.

"Hands off," Diego ordered, and Aaron's finger fell away from my face. He winked and stood, returning to Diego's side.

"We'll move tonight, dog," Aaron said. "We don't want to kill you yet, so we'll let your body heal for the night."

Diego pulled a bottle of water out of his back pocket and tossed it on the ground. It rolled above my head. I continued to stare at them, even though the thought of a drink of water nearly made me insane with need. They stared at me a few minutes longer, and when they realized I wasn't going to break, they just laughed, nudged each other, and left through the same door. They turned the lights out on their way, and I was plunged into silent darkness.

Once I knew for sure they were gone, I ignored the screaming of my body and rolled onto my other side and reached above my head, blindly searching for the cold bottle of water. When my fingers touched it, I wept with relief. I couldn't feel anything other than my need for that one drink of water. I cried out as I struggled with the lid. Fast tears rolled off my cheeks as it finally cracked open for me. I took small sips, not wanting to choke and risk wasting any of it on the floor.

After I had drunk the entire bottle, I curled into a ball, cold and crying. I had never felt so sorry for myself in my life. I missed showers. I missed clean clothes. I missed feeling warm and safe. And I missed my boys.

Where the fuck were they?

CHAPTER
three

TRISTAN

One Week Earlier

"My daughter must be one fine piece of pussy." Scarlet's father smiled a sick grin as he leaned forward and lit his cigar. He puffed a few times before leaning back and looking at all three of us. "So serious," he said as he laughed.

"This is a serious fucking matter," Seb spat at him. Could always count on Sebastian to let his anger rule his mouth. I was going to have to put a gag in it if he didn't learn how to keep his mouth shut.

Domnul Dulca raised his eyebrow at the outburst, and I knew we were found out. He might have suspected we were fucking her the last time we met, but

Seb had just outed us all in the worst way. With that little remark, he had exposed how important we thought she was.

The tension in the room was so thick you could cut it with a knife.

"Well," he said between puffs. "Like any other good dog, I'm sure she will find her way home."

"I'd honestly prefer she find her way home in one piece," I snapped back before Seb could open his mouth again. "I've already had to use my cleanup crew more than I would like to admit in the past few weeks. I'd hate to have to bring them out again. I'll have to up their pay if this shit doesn't get sorted out."

Elliot scoffed from the corner of the room, where he sat to keep an eye on everything. He was always lurking, always watching. He was the silent threat in any room. People knew he was there but rarely heard him.

"Okay, mutt," *Domnul* Dulca said, leaning forward as far as he could with his belly in the way. "If I help you with this, what do I get?"

"What do you want?"

I looked over at Seb, who had spoken out of turn again. My blood was about to boil over, and I wanted nothing more than to slap him upside the back of his head. I knew he could feel my stare on him like daggers, but he ignored me all the same. Scar's father laughed at our disorganization. In his eyes, there was weakness, a crack in the foundation of our supposed ranks. All the while his second, Mateus, sat there quietly like the obedient rat he was.

"Do you have the final say now?" he asked, looking towards Seb. "Or maybe you there, in the back? Do you sit and listen and then give little hand signals to your buddies here?" He laughed again, and I wanted to rip his jugular out to make it stop.

"I have the final say. What the fuck do you want, Dulca?"

His eyes swung back to me and narrowed at the clear disrespect in my tone. "How about a favor?" he asked with a smile.

"What kind of favor?"

"I'll decide that later on," he said, leaning back again in the chair. I could feel the atmosphere in the room change. I felt Sebastian and Elliot both go deadly silent. The only noise in the room was Dulca's heavy breathing as he sucked on that cigar in his mouth.

"I'm not going to give you that much power over us. I would be an idiot to accept those terms. Try again." Both Seb and Elliot let out collective sighs of relief. We used to be so in sync with each other, but ever since Scar went missing, we'd been slipping, making little mistakes here and there. If we didn't get our shit together, we were going to fall apart. The entire life we'd worked so hard for would go under, all because of one woman.

I sighed and tried not to let my mind go down that road. That was a dangerous path that only led to me resenting her for something that wasn't her fault. I was just angry and, honestly, a little scared that we hadn't been able to find her yet. It was putting all of us on edge. Even Elliot was grumpier than usual.

"Lift the truce, then," he said, bringing me back to the present moment. I rubbed my hands over my face and groaned. This man was really starting to get on my nerves. He was asking for impossible things, and he knew it. But I knew he was trying to see how far he could push us for Scarlet.

When I looked over at Seb, I knew he was ready to break. He was ready to give this man anything to get Scarlet back. Knowing him, he would just go on a rampage later to try and kill the entire family for trying to force our hand. It wasn't the worst idea. Elliot was stoic as ever, reclined in the chair and watching everyone intensely. His breathing was even, but only I could see the resignation in his eyes. He wanted this to be over too.

"Deal," I said and leaned forward to shake his chubby hand. He grinned and shook it with a weak grip. How that man was ever able to run a successful empire was beyond me.

"Deal," he said. "And now that all of that is taken care of, I can tell you she is being moved almost nightly. We've had an informant amongst their ranks almost since she went missing." His grin was enough to set Sebastian off. I wasn't sure if it was anger for Scarlet or anger that her father had known this whole time and just played us for the fools we very clearly were.

But Seb snapped and went right for the jugular. He was across the room in seconds, gripping Dulca by the throat and throwing him onto the floor. Dulca's men reacted at the same time Elliot and I did, pointing guns at each other and shouting orders to stand down. Seb was frozen on top of Scarlet's father while Dulca just grinned and coughed against his hand.

"Bastard," Sebastian spat down at him. "She's your own flesh and blood, and you're just going to let her rot when you could have had her out by now?" I could see his knuckles turn white out of the corner of my eye.

"Sebastian," I said in a growl. Elliot stomped out the cigar before it could light the chair on fire. *Fuck's sake*, I thought to myself. One more fucking thing that would need to be replaced. At the rate we were going, the entire house was going to have to be remodeled. But we had decided to have the meeting at the manor home for that very reason. The secret location was out, and it couldn't get any more fucked-up at this point.

"Call off your bitch, mutt!" one of Dulca's guys shouted.

"Sebastian," I tried again. "Get the fuck off of him, or he won't be around to tell us where she is."

Seb got off him with a grunt of frustration and stalked out of the room like a toddler having a tantrum. The stress of this life was going to put me in an early grave before someone could even try to do the job themselves.

I watched Dulca struggle to get his body off the ground. When he finally stood, he straightened his jacket and looked at his ruined cigar with disdain. He motioned for his men to put down their weapons, and we followed suit. I just wanted him to tell me where she was so that I could get them out of my house and get her back.

"Apologies for the outburst," I said. "We're all a bit

on edge. We just want to know where she's being held and where she is being taken and when. That way we can go get our property back."

He reached out his hand to one of the men beside him, and they handed him a piece of paper. He walked over to me and calmly placed the piece of paper in the pocket of my suit before looking up at me.

"Pleasure doing business with you, mutt. If you find her and she's still alive, please tell her that her dear father misses her, will you? She'll be at that next location in a week."

Elliot walked up to my back as we watched them leave the room. I waited until I heard the door shut before pulling the piece of paper out of my pocket and opening it. It had her current location and her next planned location on it.

"That's at least a three-hour drive away from here. And that next one is even further away," he said, reading the piece of paper over my shoulder.

"Trying to get her at her current location is too risky. We need to scout out the next place, get a plan in order, and make sure we don't fuck it up. Make some calls and get the guys together. I want to meet immediately to start making a game plan. I'm going to knock Seb around a bit before we get going."

"Don't hurt him too badly," Elliot laughed. "We'll need him at full capacity when it's time to get her back."

I rolled and cracked my neck as I left Elliot to get the men together. Sebastian was really, really pushing my limits, and even though we tried to make things as even as possible between all three of us, he needed to remember his place when it came to public transactions.

"Sebastian!" I yelled as I stalked up the stairs. He had been spending every waking and sleeping moment in Scar's room, so I had a good idea of where to find him. When I opened her door, I found him lying on her bed, playing with a switchblade and staring at the ceiling. I walked up to him and slapped him across the face.

"What was that shit about?" I asked when he didn't react other than moving his gaze from the ceiling to me and back again.

"Sorry," he said flatly.

"Sure you are. Let's go. We're meeting with Niko and the others to get a game plan together. Get your ass up."

"And if she isn't alive?" he asked quietly.

"She is."

"You don't know that," he said, folding his switchblade in and shoving it in his back pocket as he rolled off her bed. "If she isn't alive, I will kill anyone who so much as looked at her. I will kill everyone who was even remotely involved in this fucked-up little plan. And neither you nor Elliot can stop me." He brushed past me, shoving my shoulder with his own. His temper tantrums were about to push me over the edge. I could only take so much babysitting with my own burdens weighing me down.

"Hey," I said, grabbing his arm. Before I was able to register him moving, he spun around and punched me. It was hard enough that I tasted blood, and my head swung hard to the side.

"Do not fucking touch me right now." His chest was heaving with anger. I hadn't seen him this hotheaded since I first met him. "Do not try to calm me down. Do not speak down to me like I'm one of your little cronies. I'm an equal third of this fucked-up life we've all created together, and I will not be talked down to. Our girl is missing, and I'm over trying to pretend like everything is okay. We should have found her by now."

"You *are* an equal third of this," I said, getting in his face, our noses practically touching. "And that is the only reason I'm not knocking you flat on your ass for that sucker punch you just threw. Get your shit together, Sebastian," I growled as I shoved a finger against his chest. "You need your fucking head on straight. Scarlet needs you at your best. Understood?"

He shoved me away and stalked out of the room. We were all going to be so fucked if we didn't get her back alive.

CHAPTER *four*

SCARLET

The Present

They were moving me. I was swaying in and out of consciousness as someone lifted me off the ground and over their shoulder in another fireman's carry. My broken ribs screamed at the new pressure forced on them. I cried out, but it just earned me a laugh and a hard smack on the ass.

"Don't touch me," I gritted out against the pain radiating through my body.

"Feisty, this one," I heard him say before I blacked out.

I woke up once when I was thrown into the boot of a car and again when they were taking me out. At least

I thought that's what was happening. Everything in my brain was so fuzzy from lack of food and water and the constant agony I was in that I couldn't really process what was real and what wasn't.

I wanted to be weak and give up. All I could think about was curling up with Seb or Tristan playing with my hair. Shit, even Elliot's scowl would be a welcome sight. It had been so long since I had been touched with any amount of kindness that I was pretty sure I would fall apart the moment I saw them. If I ever saw them again.

God, where the fuck were they?

I was thrown down onto another hard floor unceremoniously. My vision went fuzzy and black as I blinked back the tears. I might have considered myself a tough woman, but this shit was rough. After weeks—I thought it had been weeks anyway—of torture and malnutrition, I was close to breaking.

Looking up at the men who had dropped me to the floor, I watched as a black shadow moved behind them. I blinked a few more times, trying to clear my vision, but I couldn't make it out. And then it was gone, like I had imagined the entire thing. Which I probably had considering I was so close to dying from dehydration. I was more than capable of hallucinating at this point.

I tried looking around the room, but it was poorly lit and didn't look like anything more than a basement with concrete block walls, damp and moldy. The floor I was lying on was also concrete and so cold I could feel it seeping into my bones, making my muscles and joints stiff and painful.

When was the last time I had peed? And when I did, did I pee myself? Or had they given me a bucket or a trip to the toilet? I couldn't remember. I really hoped I wasn't just lying in soiled clothes.

The man that had dropped me on the floor spat on my face, and I rolled away from them, hoping they would find me less entertaining if I just didn't interact. Maybe they would leave me the fuck alone for once. I wiped the spit from my nose and cheek as I rolled over and swallowed against the pain in my throat.

Being treated like this was wearing on me more than just physically. I could feel my sanity failing me more with each day I was stuck. I found myself praying for death as unconsciousness came for me each night. The guys obviously weren't coming for me. Either that, or the assholes who took me were just too good at keeping me hidden.

"Sleep tight, bitch," one of the men said with an accent. I realized early on that when they insulted me, they wanted to make sure I could hear them and understand them. When they spoke Spanish, it was stuff they actually wanted to be kept secret. But they wanted to wear my mind and body down. They wanted me to know when they were calling me names to make me feel like even less of a human.

The door at the top of the stairs slammed shut, and my entire body flinched with the sound. And then all I could hear was my heartbeat and my breathing. It was like being underwater. When I heard their footsteps above me echo through the room and I knew I was truly alone, I let myself cry.

They had turned the lights off when they left, cloaking me in darkness that was so black it made me feel claustrophobic. They kept doing that, putting me in this isolating darkness that made me lose track of time. I squeezed my eyes shut and willed my breath to be even. If I was going to be stuck in this hellhole until they moved me again, I was going to have to get used to the all-consuming darkness.

The tears poured hot and fast over my cheeks and temples and into my matted hair. My nose started to run, and the pain in my throat spread into my chest, making it hard to breathe. I was so weak physically that even just crying took it out of me. I was gasping and choking when a warm hand slid over my mouth. I tried to scream, but their fingers gripped into my cheeks.

"Shh, it's me, *scrumpo*." The Romanian word for "precious" rolled sweetly off his tongue. "It's Tristan. It's me." His voice was soothing and warm, and I turned around to face him so quickly that my ribs screamed in pain, but I ignored them. I felt him move to sit next to me on the ground, picking me up into his lap as I curled my body into his. My hands and arms were all over him, making sure he was real and alive and not just a hallucination my brain had conjured up.

He held me gently, murmuring soothing sounds in my ear as I wept into his chest and neck, breathing in the clean scent of him. I couldn't imagine what I smelled like, but he held me to him like it was nothing. He whispered against my hair, petting and kissing it like I was something to be cherished.

"Fuck, I missed you," he said when my breathing

had returned to normal. "I thought we had lost you, poppet."

"How are you here? Where are the boys?" I asked, pulling away to try and get a glimpse of his face. I wouldn't believe all of this was real until I could see him. I needed to see him. My dirty hands found his face, and I tried to remember what he looked like, but my mind was just a blank slate. There was a piece of cloth wrapped around the lower half of his face, and I yanked it away, running my fingertips over his mouth.

"Long story, baby," he said, pulling my hands away from his face so that he could lean in and kiss me. I had forgotten how soft his lips were. His hands were back in my hair, holding my face to his as his tongue explored my mouth. He was drinking me in and stealing my breath. "The guys are outside. We'll hear them any minute now. Seb is going to hand out death like the grim reaper to get to you."

I smiled against his lips as I kissed him again.

"Can you walk?" he asked.

"I'm not sure, honestly," I answered, knowing his plan to rescue me was going to be a lot harder if I couldn't help them help me. "I haven't had to walk in a long time. I'm either lying down while they beat me, or they're carrying me to and from a car boot." His grip on my hair tightened, pulling at my scalp. "I can try though."

I thought about how I was missing toenails and wondered if I would be able to stand the excruciating pain that was going to cause as I ran through god knew what to get out. It would be so much easier if one of them was able to carry me.

"No," he said firmly. "You aren't going to risk hurting yourself even more. I can carry you, okay? I texted them we were in the basement before I followed you guys down here, so they're going to get us when it's safe."

As he finished that sentence, gunshots and shouting started above us. Heavy footsteps pounded on the floor above our heads, and muffled screaming could be heard in both English and Spanish.

"We need to move against the wall in case anyone comes down here to check on you, okay? I need to make sure I can put myself between you and them." He lifted me in his arms and slowly stood before taking cautious steps towards a corner of the room. Once we bumped into the walls, he sat me down on the floor, and I tried not to protest at the searing hot pain that had rippled through my body.

I felt him box me in with his body before he placed a gun in my hand. More and more gunshots were going off upstairs, and the adrenaline that began coursing through my body helped numb the pain and exhaustion. I was so close to getting out. I was so close to being safe with my boys again.

Suddenly, the beginning notes of "Back in Black" by AC/DC could be heard through the walls, getting closer and closer to where we were. I felt myself smile for the first time in weeks.

"Sebastian," Tristan said on a sigh before I could ask. "He thought you would find it funny."

I burst out laughing, holding my aching ribs in one hand and gripping the gun in the other. I leaned forward and laid my forehead on Tristan's jean-clad leg.

"These guys are so fucked."

The cavalry had arrived. And these assholes had no idea who they had fucked with.

CHAPTER
five

SEBASTIAN

Present

They were so severely underprepared it was humorous. I was taking out men left and right. Hell, we wouldn't have even had to call in our guys to help. They were dropping like flies, and I was a kid in a fucking candy store. Blood and brain matter exploded from every guy I took down. We needed to do this shit more often, I thought to myself. It was a high I hadn't experienced in too long.

Elliot was shouting something at me, but I couldn't hear him over my phone blasting AC/DC out of my pocket. Elliot and Tristan had fought me on the idea before we had left the house, but if Scarlet was alive, I knew she would appreciate it.

And she was alive.

We had watched her get pulled and lifted out of the car boot before being thrown over the shoulder of some soon-to-be-dead asshole. Once they had her inside, Tristan had snuck in behind them, leaving me and Elliot to command our men and make sure we got them both out alive.

I was a man on a fucking mission in that house. The number one rule I told the men was to make sure my ass was covered. Because my plan was to storm into that place and make my way directly to Scar, and I was going to kill anyone that got in my line of sight.

With a gun in each hand, I shot everyone I crossed paths with, opening every door I came across until one opened into the basement. Suddenly, I saw someone coming up on me out of the corner of my eye. I went to shoot, but both of my guns clicked with empty rounds. I was so distracted thinking about finding her that I had lost count of my rounds. Thank fuck he was empty-handed as well. Hand-to-hand combat it was.

"Come on, then, sweetness. I don't have all night," I said with a smile.

He swung, and I ducked, coming back up with a punch directly to his chin. His head went flying back as I grabbed his shoulders and kneed him in the balls. He crumpled to the floor in a heap of moaning man meat. I stepped back and kicked him hard across the face, watching in sheer delight as his blood and teeth went flying across the floor. His jaw was hanging from his skull at an awkwardly limp angle. I squatted next to him and pulled the switchblade out of my back pocket.

"I don't know if you touched her or if you even looked at her," I said down to him as his face rolled back to face me. He was half-delirious with pain. "But I'm going to err on the side of caution and say you probably have. So…I'm going to kill you now." I smiled and shoved the blade into the side of his neck. Blood gushed from the wound and sprayed across my hand.

Good. I needed some more blood on me to make my girl proud.

"Seb?" I heard her voice come from behind me. I turned towards her and ran my bloody hands through my hair. It had gotten longer in those few weeks without her.

I took in her tiny figure. She looked like a small child in Tristan's arms. Her normally shiny, healthy hair was matted and tangled. Her skin had lost all its glow. She was pale with bruises across every inch of flesh I could see, with deep purple bags under her eyes. Blood was smeared and dried across her face, and her bright blue eyes were dull and heavy-lidded.

But that smile? Fuck me, that smile was the same I had seen that night before we had laid down in bed together. It was what had consumed my every waking thought. It haunted my dreams every night as I lay in her bed, smelling her fresh scent. I never wanted to go without it again.

"AC/DC?" she asked, her grin growing wider as her eyes skated over my body. I puffed my chest out a bit and winked at her, holding myself back from running to her and ripping her out of Tristan's arms. The need to feel her warm body was all-consuming, but I could see in the way she flinched with each step up from the basement that she was in pain. Tristan was holding her as gently as possible and walking slowly so as to not jostle her, but her body was in awful condition.

"I thought it set the mood, princess," I answered her as they came to the top of the steps.

"I'd reach for you, but I think a few of my ribs are broken, and moving hurts. Like, really fucking hurts." Tears started to stream down her cheeks. It was killing me to see her so broken.

"It's okay, pet," I said as I closed the distance between us. I leaned in, restraining every instinct in my body to grab her and rut her into the ground, and gave her a soft kiss on the mouth. I wiped her tears away. "Let's get you out of here, yeah?"

"Yeah," she said, curling herself a bit more into Tristan's body.

"Let's go!" Elliot yelled from the front room. "Get her in the car. We'll finish up here!"

"Hi, Grumpy!" she squealed when they made it closer to Elliot. He just grunted in return, but he couldn't stop the smile from growing. Stupid fucker needed to nut up and join the Scarlet fan club.

I watched them leave the house, seeing absolute bloody red rage for what they had done to her. They took our vibrant, carefree girl and made her feel broken and helpless. But we would show her that wasn't true. We would get her back on her feet, help her heal, and make her feel whole again.

It was kind of disappointing that I had killed everyone so quickly. It would've been so much more satisfying if I had been able to choke the life out of each and every one of them. But after how many of their people I had killed since they took her, they were definitely feeling the dent in their numbers, and that's what mattered. We were taking down their entire operation. If they didn't know who they were dealing with when they first took her, they were definitely starting to learn their lesson.

"Is that everyone, El?" I asked.

"Lads are checking around to make sure no one was missed, but yeah. Seems like we got everyone." He walked down the corridor and pulled my phone out of my back pocket, turning off the music that was still blasting before handing it back to me. I grinned at him when he shook his head. "You look psychotic. You're covered in blood. Jesus Christ, Seb. Get your shit together."

I tilted my head at his tone. He was always an ass, but he had really taken a turn in the last few weeks. I thought once we found Scarlet, he might loosen up a little bit. But I had been patient for as long as I could stand it. I had already knocked him out once, and I really didn't feel like starting another fight. But he was walking on thin fucking ice with me.

"Problem, Elliot?"

"I'm just a little bit sick of being shot at over a girl."

"A girl…" I drawled, narrowing my eyes on him. "You need to get over whatever shit you have going on in there," I said, tapping his forehead. "Because she is clearly important to both me and Tristan. I thought before all this went down, you were starting to feel something for her too. Even now, when she was excited to see you, you smiled."

"Fuck off, Seb. I'm not going to get gooey-eyed over a piece of pussy."

He went to push past me, but I laughed and stepped into his way. This really wasn't the fucking day. He glared at me and crossed his arms. He was an intimidating fucker, but I wasn't going to let him get away with talking about Scarlet with the same tone her father spoke about her. Even if he didn't like her, she deserved respect.

"You don't get to talk about her like that, Elliot."

"Get. The fuck. Out of. My way."

I laughed again and, before he could see it coming, kneed him right in the balls like I had done to the poor sucker on the floor next to us. Normally I wouldn't have taken such a cheap shot, but honestly, he deserved it. Elliot doubled over, coughing and his face turning red. I smiled and watched as he fell to his knees on the floor.

"I'll let you recover while I round up the guys and make sure they're out of here before we torch it. Make sure you're out too. I'm not coming back to check."

CHAPTER
six

SCARLET

Present Day

"Hey, sweet cheeks," Seb said as he gingerly sat in the back seat with me and lifted my head onto his lap. The car smelled like all three of my boys, clean with a hint of their spicy cologne. It was so comforting that I had fallen asleep the moment Tristan had laid me down.

"Hey, handsome." My voice came out scratchy and quiet. I looked up at him and admired his dark eyes. Their usual playfulness was gone, replaced by worry and fatigue. My cinnamon roll was exhausted. He looked hollow and pained.

"We're taking you to a new safe house, okay? It's going to be a long drive, and I know you probably feel gross, but we don't want to take the chance of being seen." His hands soothed through my tangled hair, and I winced as it pulled at my scalp. "Sorry," he said as he recoiled like I had bitten him.

"Hey," I said, moving slowly to take his hand in my own. I kissed the palm and breathed him in. Even the scent of blood on his hands comforted me. My boys had finally found me. Seb had killed people to get to me, but he was being so gentle with me it made my heart ache. I wasn't used to this sad, quiet side of him.

"I'm sorry, Scarlet," he admitted, brushing his thumb over my lips.

"We all are, princess," Tristan said from the front seat. "We were fighting every single day to get back to you."

"It tore us apart," Seb whispered.

"It's okay," I assured them both as I kissed Seb's palm again. "I'm with you guys now. Better than being dead, right?" I tried to laugh it off, but Seb's face was bleak. "Where are we going?" I asked to change the subject.

"North," Elliot answered as he got into the driver's seat and slammed the door. I winced at the noise, my head already pounding.

"A little fucking tact, Elliot," Sebastian growled.

"I'll have a little fucking tact when my balls stop aching."

Sebastian laughed, and I saw Tristan turn around to look at him out of the corner of my eye. Seb shrugged and looked back down at me, brushing my hair out of my face and playing with it in a way that wouldn't cause it to pull against my scalp.

"So I have to wait until we get to this safe house before I can bathe?" I yawned and closed my eyes, relishing the fact that I could do that without being terrified that someone was going to sneak up on me for the first time in weeks. I always felt safer, even from my own nightmares, when Seb was sleeping with me, but it felt even more important now for one of them to always be with me, just in case.

And I wasn't going to let my pride get in the way of that.

"Unfortunately," Elliot mumbled as he started the car.

"Your balls won't be the only thing aching if you don't watch your mouth," Tristan told him.

"Yes, baby," Seb cooed down at me. "I know you must feel dirty, but we just can't risk stopping, okay?"

I nodded and fought back the tears. I didn't really know why I wanted to cry again. It could've been the relief I felt at finally being safe, or it could've been the way Elliot was talking to me again, like I was as annoying as gum on the bottom of his shoe.

I thought we had made a little bit of progress, but the way he was acting made me think maybe we hadn't. I dreaded the thought of starting all over again with him. Seb wiped the tears away from my face that had escaped, and I looked up at his soft smile.

"We will help you take a shower the moment we get there, okay, princess?" Tristan turned around and asked.

All I could manage was a small nod.

"Baby," Seb said in a soft voice. "Something else happened the night you were taken, and it doesn't feel right to hide it from you."

"Sebastian!" Tristan yelled, causing me to jump and bump my broken ribs. I groaned and shuffled further into Seb. "We talked about this!"

"You talked. I didn't listen."

"Just fucking tell her and get it over with," Elliot grumbled. "She may as well know about the destruction she left in her wake."

"It was not her fucking fault," Seb growled back, cradling my head against his abs like he could protect my ears like a small child. "We talked about this. We talked about you not being a cunt and getting your head out of your ass."

"You talked. I didn't listen," Elliot shot back.

"Oh, you know what, Elliot? Get fucked. Pull this fucking car over and let me show you how badly I can make those tiny shriveled ba—"

"Seb!" I interrupted, seeing as Tristan obviously had stopped playing referee since I got taken. Jesus, was everything between them fucked? "Just fucking tell me what happened!"

He sighed and looked down at me. "So the reason I left you that night was because we got a call that there was some shit going down at the loft," Seb said. "Turns out, it was just a diversion to get us all out of the house so that you were left vulnerable. But they did actually destroy the loft and…" He trailed off. Even in the dim light of the car, I could see his eyes were wet. I gingerly reached up and stroked his cheek.

I might have been going through hell, but clearly something had happened to my boys as well.

"What happened, love?" I asked him.

He sighed and looked out the window, away from me. The anxiety was making my pulse pound in my ears. If someone didn't tell me what happened soon, broken ribs and missing toenails be damned, I was going to punch someone.

"Mel is gone, Scarlet." Seb's voice cracked, and he viciously wiped at his face, abandoning touching any part of my body in comfort.

"What?" I asked, dread filling my stomach.

Not Mel.

"Yeah," Elliot chimed in from the front as he took a turn a little too fast. "Mel was shot and killed in cold blood all because of you."

"Elliot," Tristan said in a warning tone.

"If you don't shut the *fuck* up, Elliot," Seb started, his arms wrapping protectively around me again. "And you," he said, directing his anger at Tristan. "If I didn't have *my* broken girl on my lap, I would teach you a lesson too. Because the way you're both acting is insane. None of this is Scarlet's fault, and I will *not* let you blame her for this shit. It's pathetic."

I swallowed against the pain in my throat. I would not cry again. They were hurt. They had a right to be upset. Ignoring the pain in my ribs, I half sat up and crawled onto Seb. He helped me get situated, and I tucked my face into his neck as he cradled me.

"I'm so sorry," I whispered. He turned and kissed my forehead before holding me tighter to him.

"Oh, she's yours now?" Tristan turned around and asked, a playful grin on his face. I didn't think Seb was in the mood to play though.

"She's mine and only mine until you both get your heads out of your asses and earn her back."

CHAPTER
seven

ELLIOT

Present Day

I was tired.

I was tired of driving, of the tension in the car, and of hearing Scarlet's fucking snores for the past five hours.

"Doctor will be there first thing in the morning," Tristan whispered into the silence of the car. We didn't even have the music on so that the precious thing could sleep.

I nodded at Tristan and continued staring straight ahead. I could hear him hesitate, wanting to ask me what was going on in my head, but he thought better of it. Good for him. I wasn't in the mood.

Truth was, I didn't really blame Scarlet for this shit. Well, not completely anyway. Would we have been in the mess we were if we had never taken her in? Probably not. But was it actually her fault that Mel was gone? I didn't think so. I was just having a really hard time keeping my emotions in check.

Her absence had broken something between all of us. We ended up taking all of our shit out on each other instead of letting it bring us together. I didn't know why we had reacted like that. It should've been something that banded us together, but it hadn't, and that had also pissed me off.

It was like this thing that we had worked to build with each other over so many years was so easily threatened, all because none of us knew how to charter these new waters. So I didn't know who to blame.

Did I blame her family for treating her so badly that she ran away, giving us the opportunity to track her down? Did I blame her for convincing Seb and Tristan to keep her? Did I blame myself for leaving her that night?

I sighed and gripped the steering wheel as I made our way through the quiet neighborhood.

"Thinking awfully loudly, El," Tristan said, never lifting his eyes from his phone screen. I glanced back at Seb and Scarlet in the rearview. They were both still sound asleep, Seb holding on to her like a life raft. It was going to take the force of God himself to get him to let her out of his sight now. That sick feeling of jealousy rolled through me. I hated feeling jealous of what they had with her.

"A lot to think about," I finally answered.

"That there is," he sighed, stuffing his phone in his pocket as we pulled up to one of my old family safe houses in the middle of suburbia. The papers were signed over to a random no-name when my father passed, and the paper trail burned. It was all of our hopes, especially mine, that the assholes wouldn't think to look right under their noses for her.

I had somehow convinced the other two that this location also needed to be kept a secret from Scarlet. Because even after I saw how beat to shit she was, I still couldn't shake the doubt. The doubt that maybe she wasn't one hundred percent innocent in all of this. It had made Seb go psycho on me last week when I brought it up. My jaw was still sore from where he had sucker punched me.

I didn't care what they thought of me for suspecting her. I was the only one thinking with the head up top and not the one below the belt. It would suit her father perfectly to have her on the inside with us, sleeping her way through each one of us, gaining our trust and secrets. And I wouldn't put it past her dad to let them kick the shit out of her to make it look real.

"Hey, princess," Tristan murmured to her, leaning between the seats and stroking her thigh. She jumped awake and then let out a scream at the pain that movement caused. Seb was instantly awake and shushing her while rocking her in his arms as she cried.

"I'm sorry. I'm sorry," she kept saying over and over again through her tears. Tristan glanced over at me, worry etched clearly on his face. I hid mine by rolling my eyes and climbing out of the parked car.

I breathed deeply, the icy cold air waking me up. I stretched and rolled my neck before opening the boot and pulling out all of the duffle bags, letting them hit the concrete with dull thuds. The house was relatively well stocked, but there definitely wasn't anything there for Scarlet to wear. Seb had packed her a bag filled with brand-new clothes he just had to buy for her. I picked up my own two bags, deliberately leaving the rest out of spite.

"Let's go," I said through the boot and then closed it quietly, hoping not to wake anyone at the neighboring houses. They weren't connected, but it was a small cul-de-sac in the middle of nowhere, and it was well before dawn. I figured it might be a good idea to not draw attention to ourselves by pissing off the neighbors.

I unlocked the front door and walked in, turning off the alarms and flipping on the lights as I looked around. I did a quick sweep through the house while Seb carried Scarlet into the foyer.

Scarlet gripped onto Sebastian's neck so tightly I could see her knuckles turning white. Her face was pale and slightly green. In the dim light of the front hallway, she looked even worse than I remembered. Her hair was extremely matted, to the point I wasn't sure we would ever get the knots out. She was absolutely covered in blood, and as they walked past me, I could smell the sweat and urine on her.

They definitely hadn't taken it easy on her. Had she

not even been allowed a bucket to piss in? *Christ.* Tristan walked in behind them, bogged down with all the bags, glaring at me as he dropped them on the floor.

"You're the biggest of all of us, and yet you only carried two bags inside?" he asked.

"I was taking on all the risk of being attacked as the first one inside," I answered with a smirk I knew would piss him off. "I needed my hands." I shrugged.

He watched as Seb adjusted his grip on Scar's body before they walked up the skinny flight of stairs. The house wasn't anything like the manor or the loft. It wasn't some big ostentatious show of wealth. From the outside, it looked like your normal family home. But what no one could see was how it had a fortress of a basement and cameras that covered every angle, inside and out.

"You're trying to make this as hard as possible on everyone, aren't you?" Tristan asked as he shut the door.

"I'm keeping my distance and therefore my fucking sanity. I can't be around Seb when he's like this."

"You mean you can't be around her when she's like this." He put his hand on my shoulder and squeezed as he walked towards the back of the house.

He was right. I couldn't be around her when she looked at me like she had when we saved her.

She looked at me like I'd hung the damn moon. I couldn't stand to see her have any sort of affection for me. Not when I was still worried she could be a plant. She had started to get under my skin before she disappeared, and when I saw her in Tristan's arms coming from the basement, I could feel that relief all too easily.

If I got close to her now that we had her back, I'd cave. I needed to stay cold and distant and keep my eyes open for the next thing to come our way. I sighed, resisting the urge to punch a hole in the wall, and made my way to the garage to take my aggression out in the gym before I took it out on her.

CHAPTER
eight

SCARLET

Falling asleep in Seb's arms on the way to the safe house was the best sleep I'd had in weeks. Did I wake up with my neck in a funny position and every muscle in my body screaming? Yes. But the smell and feel of him was so worth it.

He gently lifted me out of the car and helped me stand up. Stretching felt wonderful and insanely painful all at the same time. He gently lifted my arm over his shoulders and scooped me up, trying as best he could to keep the pressure directly off my ribs.

It didn't look like any safe house I'd ever been to. All of my family's places were either hidden in the middle of nowhere or looked like medieval fortresses. The house in front of us was a family home. I looked behind us and saw Tristan picking up a ton of bags.

"Seb, go help him. Just put me down."

"He's fine," he said, brushing off my concern. Since I was in so much pain, I decided to let them baby me without giving them grief for once. Elliot was standing in the front hallway as we made our way inside. His eyes glanced over me with a look that bordered on disgust before Seb continued to carry me up the stairs. I couldn't blame him, I probably looked and smelled like a sewer rat.

"Let's get you a shower, pet," he whispered into my ear.

I let my head roll into the crook of his neck and inhaled.

"You smell good," I groaned as I nipped at the soft flesh there.

"Scarlet," he warned in a tone that lacked real threat.

"Sebastian," I sang back to him. "Do you know what I just realized?" We turned a tight corner and entered a fairly large bedroom and then into the adjoining bathroom.

"What's that, baby?"

"We're both going to be naked in there," I said, nodding towards the shower as he sat me down on the toilet. He turned on the water and then knelt in between my legs. His smile was enough to turn my pain into butterflies as he looked up at me.

His fingertips skimmed across my waist, pulling my shirt up until he helped me pull my arms free. Moving to the cabinet, he dug through all the stuff under the sink before pulling out a first aid kit.

"I'm going to use scissors and just cut your sports bra off, yeah? It'll hurt like a bitch to pull that off with the state you're in."

"You're kind of killing the mood here, handsome," I said, smiling at him as he cut off the straps and then straight up the middle of the bra. He peeled it off my dirty, bloody skin and let his thumbs graze over my nipples. My breathing hitched, and the pain in my chest was the last thing on my mind.

I leaned into his touch, and he took the opportunity to help me stand and pull off my old pajama shorts and soiled underwear. I probably should've had the decency to be embarrassed, but I couldn't with Seb. He was my first of the boys, the one that cared the hardest beneath his rough exterior, and I knew none of this would make him look at me any different or care for me any less.

He helped me stay upright while using his free hand to strip himself of all of his clothing. I got a thrill when he dropped his briefs and saw he was already hard, standing out proudly below the sharp vee of his hips. It was all I could do to not drop to my knees and taste him again.

"I can see what you're thinking, little one," he said as he stepped out of his boxers. "But we both need a shower."

"Fine. Spoilsport," I said, giving him a peck on the cheek before he lifted me up and carried me into the shower. He made sure I was safely on my feet before coaxing me back into the water.

God, did that feel good.

He washed my hair and conditioned it four times

before he could get all the knots out with his fingers. His hands were gentle as they explored and washed my body, the water running a rusty red at our feet. I could feel my muscles relaxing under the heat of the water and his careful ministrations.

He switched our positions, and I held on to him while he bathed himself. I couldn't lift my hands too high because of my ribs, but they could easily move across his abs and hips. He groaned as I moved lower, taking the length of him in my slippery hand and stroking him from base to tip.

"You're going to be the death of me," he said as he pushed his forehead on mine, his eyes closing and breath coming hot and fast against my lips. "You should be resting."

"I've missed you. I need this, Seb. Please," I begged. I did need it. I needed to feel close to him, to know he was really there in front of me, that he was real. "I've missed the way you sound when you come for me."

"Fuck," he swore under his breath. "I should be the bigger person here, but I'm already so close this won't last long, anyway." He gave a little laugh, and I smiled as I took his mouth in mine, tasting him and drinking him in. The water poured over our faces as his hips bucked into my hand.

"That's it, baby," I encouraged him as he broke the kiss and moaned as both my hand movements and his hips became more erratic. "Come for me." He chanted my name over and over again under his breath before coming all over my stomach and hand.

As he came down from his high, he kissed his way

across my jaw, my neck, my cheeks, and finally my mouth. I laughed as he rinsed the evidence of his orgasm away before sweeping me up into his arms again.

"Your turn, little minx."

Next thing I knew, he had thrown a towel down on the bed and laid me on top of it before descending on my pussy like a starving man. I cried out and gripped my fingers into his wet hair as he sucked my clit into his mouth and pushed a finger inside of me.

"Yes," I breathed as he continued his assault, pushing me closer and closer to the delirious edge of my orgasm. His fingers kept curling, his teeth kept nibbling, and he kept growling, making his lips vibrate against me. I couldn't catch my breath, and he just continued, pushing and curling, sucking and biting, until with a scream and a flood of heat, I came.

"That's my fucking girl," he said, cleaning me up with tortuously slow licks across every inch of my cunt. He grinned and took his fingers into his mouth, sucking them clean, before disappearing into the bathroom and coming back out with more fluffy white towels.

"Now, how about we dry you off so that you can get some sleep until the doctor comes?"

Sounded really fucking good to me.

CHAPTER
nine

SCARLET

I rolled over and groaned in pain. The bed was so soft and warm, but I was in desperate need of the toilet and more pain meds. The doctor came about an hour after I had fallen asleep. I barely remembered anything he had said to me or done other than feed me pain meds. Once he was done stitching and wrapping, I had fallen back into bed with Seb and back to sleep.

"Do you need to get up?" Seb asked in the sweetest sleepy voice.

"I do, but you're not about to help me pee, Seb," I told him as I gently tried to untangle myself from his wild limbs. Somehow in the night, he had managed to wrap me up against him like a spider in a web. A delicious web made of hard muscle and tattoos.

Focus. You have to pee.

He laughed and gently but forcibly pulled me back to him.

"I think I'd prefer to keep you here," he said, nipping at the tender skin of my neck.

"You want me to pee on you? I didn't know you were into watersports, Sebastian," I teased, still trying to move out of his grasp without breaking another rib.

"I'm down for anything you wanna try, little pet." He kissed me hard on the lips, moving his tongue across mine as I opened my mouth to him. His hands gripped my bare ass and squeezed, making me moan and move against him. He smacked my ass and then broke the kiss. "Go pee. I'll help you change your bandages and stuff after. Get some more meds in you."

After I limped and waddled to and from the bathroom, he was sitting on the edge of the bed in black boxer briefs, holding medical supplies and looking like a tattooed god. Although, he looked too much like sin to be considered a god.

"Keep looking at me like that and I won't be able to let you heal properly before I pound your tight little pussy into the mattress." He licked his lips and looked me over. There was no way I could look good to him right now covered in bruises and cuts, with slept-on hair and looking so skinny you could see every bone in my body. But he was looking at me like he wanted to devour me.

I grinned at him and lay down on the bed, letting him pull his shirt I slept in up over my body, exposing all of my wounds so that he could clean and wrap me back up.

"You know," he said as he gently peeled some bandages from my stomach, "when we couldn't find you, we kind of fell apart." He glanced up at me before continuing his work.

"What do you mean?" I asked, trying and failing to sit up on my elbows so that I could get a better look at him. I lifted my head as best I could to see what he was doing. The sadness was back in his eyes, and he refused to look up at me anymore.

"We were at each other's throats the entire time. I was speaking out of turn, Elliot was grumpier than usual, and Tristan made…questionable decisions." He sighed. "It was like none of us knew how to navigate losing you. We didn't know how to talk to each other anymore, which is so stupid considering you had only been around for such a short time and we had been alone for years before you."

I laid my head back down, blinking against the tears that were threatening to fall, and reached a hand out to him. He lay down next to my side, and I guided his head to my chest. I didn't care how sore I was; I wanted to feel his weight on me. I ran my hands through his soft hair. He had let it get a bit longer since I saw him last, and I kind of liked it.

"I'm so sorry, Seb. About all of it. I'm so sorry that you guys lost Mel."

"Hey," he said, sitting up and looking down on me. "It is not your fault that we left you alone that night, and it definitely isn't your fault that your family is a piece of shit. I didn't want to leave you that night. I should've fought harder to stay."

He leaned down and kissed me again, this time with purpose. He forced my mouth open to his and stole my breath. We poured everything we couldn't say out loud into that kiss. Warmth pooled low in my stomach, and I begged him with my body to keep going. I needed it. I needed the distraction and the connection to another human being. I needed to be grounded with him. His fingers gently trailed across my stomach and over my hips, settling in between my thighs as he nudged them apart.

"I've missed your moans," he said as he peppered kisses across my jaw and brushed a fingertip over my clit. I gasped and pushed my hips up to get more friction. "Be a good girl and let me take care of you, okay?" he whispered. "Lie here and let me do all the work."

"Good morning!" Tristan announced as he strutted into the room. Seb rolled off me and groaned. I felt about the same at being interrupted but smiled when I saw Tristan carrying a tray filled with food. My stomach was instantly growling.

"Oh my god," I moaned and tried to sit up so I could shove my face full.

"My sentiments exactly," Seb murmured before assisting me and propping me up on every pillow available.

"Keep it in your pants, Seb. She just got back."

"She started it," Sebastian said before giving me a quick peck on the lips. "I'll go shower while you eat." Then he turned to Tristan with a serious face. "She needs new bandages and her pain pills. I'll be back in a minute."

Tristan stood there, holding the tray piled high with food, and watched Sebastian leave with an eyebrow raised. I laughed when he turned back towards me, holding my ribs against the pain. Tristan gave his head a little shake and then gently laid the tray over my legs.

"He's really on one, isn't he? Like a kid with a toy."

"Hi," I said as he sat down next to me. His face softened, and he leaned forward to kiss me.

"Hi, poppet." He leaned back and looked at me, taking in all of my stitches and bruises. I grabbed his hand and squeezed it before making a dramatic show of how hungry I was.

"I'm going to eat literally every single pastry, slab of bacon, and piece of fruit on this tray. And don't even think about touching any of these pancakes."

"Wouldn't dream of it, love," he said, smiling and then moving to lean against the headboard next to me. I looked around the tray and didn't see any coffee, only juice and water.

"No coffee?" I asked him with an exaggerated pout on my lips. His green eyes sparkled before he grabbed my lower lip with a soft bite.

"Not until you're properly hydrated, doctor's orders. Eat, and then you can go back to letting Seb give you so many orgasms you sleep for days."

I leaned over and rested my head on his shoulder as I grabbed a slice of bacon and relished in the salty taste. God, I had missed food. Looking at the overflowing tray, I knew I wouldn't be able to eat it all after going for a couple of weeks with only a drink of water here and there. But damn, I wanted to eat everything he offered me.

"I'm sorry about Mel, Tris," I said quietly into the silence. He turned and kissed my hair.

"I don't blame you, poppet." I felt his lips move against my head. "Neither does Elliot," he sighed. "He just needs some time to sort out his shit, okay?"

I nodded and turned my attention back to the tray while Tristan plaited my hair out of my face. After he was pleased with his work, he got my meds and instructed me to take them before hauling off the tray of food that was only half-eaten. I felt sick and bloated but so, so happy.

"Thank you." I smiled at him while he made sure I had clean bandages.

"Anything for you, Scarlet." He kissed me hard, pushing my mouth open with his tongue and kissing me like he thought he'd never get the chance again. "And if I wasn't worried Sebastian would separate my head from my body," he said with a laugh, "I would take over the job of giving you orgasms for the day. But I won't be denying him anything for a while."

I smiled and kissed him again, threading my hands through his soft hair before Sebastian interrupted us like a helicopter mom. He cleared his throat and leaned against the doorframe, his arms crossed and face serious.

"Sebastian," I groaned playfully. "Leave him alone. He brought me breakfast and dressed my wounds."

"Yeah, and I gave you an orgasm that sent you into a stupor."

"Is that a challenge?" Tristan asked with a smirk on his face. He stood and took the tray with him as he walked over to Seb. "Because I'll go toe to toe with you, Seb, and I don't think you'll like the outcome." He leaned in quickly and noisily kissed him on the cheek. I laughed, and Seb made a show of wiping it off and then smacking Tristan's ass as he left.

"Your turn," he said, turning to face me. He closed the door with his foot and then sprinted and jumped onto the bed next to me, narrowly avoiding colliding with my body. I was laughing so hard I thought I would break another rib. But it was worth it. It felt good to finally be back with my boys, safe and loved…for the time being, anyway.

CHAPTER
ten

TRISTAN

"They shouldn't be fucking around," Elliot grumbled from the couch across from me. I was in a bit of a mood myself, mainly because I was jealous that it was Seb that got her first. Not that I was that surprised. He was the first one to fall for her, and he was the first one she fell for. I scrubbed my hands over my face and through my hair.

"Elliot," I started, taking a deep breath.

"Don't fucking start," he said, getting up and stomping out of the room.

"Okay, then," I said to the empty room. A moment later, Seb walked down the stairs, hair sticking up at all angles and a smile on his face.

"Pleased with yourself?" I asked him as he plopped

himself down onto the couch Elliot had just abandoned.

"Very," he answered. "Was she that loud?" He looked over at me with a shit-eating grin.

"You know she was." I closed my laptop and couldn't hold back the laugh at just how pleased he was with himself. No matter how jealous I was that he got to taste her first, I was relieved to see him smile again. "How's she doing? Sleeping again?"

"Yeah. She's hurting, mentally and physically. But she's doing better than I expected." He chewed on his thumb and then looked over at me with a mischievous smile. "I think the multiple orgasms helped."

I stood up and put my laptop down on the coffee table.

"We have shit to discuss," I told him as I walked past him and into the kitchen to make another cup of coffee. I was on my fourth of the day, trying to get through planning our next steps with her family and whoever it was that had taken her.

"I figured you already had a plan, and Elliot and I would just fall in line," he said with a bite in his tone, following me into the kitchen.

"Despite the way we've been acting the last couple weeks, we're still a team, and I would prefer for us all to be on board before we jump into anything. Maybe if we decide on a plan that Elliot is okay with, it'll help his sour-ass mood."

"Alright," he said, hopping up on a barstool. "What's your idea, then?"

"Well, the first thing is to not let our territory go

unguarded for too long. We need to get back to London before her family decides to just take over. It worries me, us all being here."

"Niko and the others can handle it," Seb said, shaking an empty mug towards me. I rolled my eyes and took it from him to make him a cup as well. "They're more than capable of handling that shit. Next problem."

"They may be more than capable of handling rival gang members, but that doesn't mean we should make them deal with it on their own, and it definitely doesn't mean they can handle the big guys. We should at least plan to pop in every once in a while until this shit is over with to keep Dulca on his toes. If you think he won't try shit just because we aren't there, you're delusional."

"We aren't leaving her here alone," he volleyed back.

"I never said we would." I didn't want to leave her alone either. Even if she was safe in a tiny village in the middle of nowhere, she wasn't going to be left out of our sight ever again.

"I'll stay." I looked up and saw Elliot standing in the doorway. Seb let out a loud cackle that I wanted to mirror. The last of us I would have thought would volunteer would be Elliot. I also would've been lying if I said it didn't worry me to leave them alone together. Seb and I could come back to the house being burnt to the ground and them fighting to the death.

"Why do you want to stay?" I asked him, suspicion heavy in my voice.

"Because Scarlet and I have some shit we need to work out. Just me and her. I'd prefer us not have an audience for it."

"Yeah, that's going to be a hell no from me, mate," Seb said, laughing to himself. His back was to Elliot, and I looked between the two of them. Honestly, it would make more sense for Elliot to go with me. He was the supposed brawn of the operation, and Scarlet had always been more comfortable with Sebastian.

But if we left her and Elliot alone to get their shit out in the open, maybe he would finally get over himself and they could fuck it out.

It also wouldn't hurt to have Seb's particular set of gifts with me in case something went wrong. Elliot could fight anyone that came our way, but Seb... Seb was his own brand of crazy. He wouldn't let anyone get in the way of him getting home to Scarlet.

He finally realized I had been quiet for too long and looked up at me.

"T, no," he said, his temper suddenly rising. "You said we wouldn't do anything that wasn't a unanimous decision."

"You want to keep Scarlet, yes?" I asked him.

"Dumb question."

"If you want to keep her and have her be as happy as she can, you need to let her and Elliot work out their shit." I looked at Elliot out of the corner of my eye and saw him smirking. I was just glad Sebastian couldn't see the look on his face. If he turned around and saw the thoughts written all over Elliot's face, he'd never leave them alone again. Whatever it was he had planned, I had a feeling it would end up working out whether he intended it to or not.

"And," I continued, "if someone is going to stay with her, it makes sense that it would be the bodyguard of the group, yes? Wouldn't that make sense from the outside looking in?"

Seb looked up at me, angry resignation in his eyes. He was going to give in to the idea, but he wasn't thrilled about it. He popped his knuckles and then rolled his neck before jumping off the stool and going to stand in Elliot's face.

"I will not hesitate to knock you out again if you hurt her."

Elliot just smiled at him.

"Mentally, emotionally, or physically?" he asked. I groaned and prepared myself to have to break up another fight.

"Look," I said, walking over to push them away from each other. "We have her back. Can you two please chill the fuck out?" I gave Seb a little shove back, and he let me, taking the opportunity to circle the island and stare Elliot down from there.

"So Elliot will stay here with Scarlet," I said. "Next hurdle to tackle is going to be what the fuck we are going to do with whoever is behind this shit." I made my way back over to the counter to fill up my coffee and Sebastian's. "We really need to figure out if her family was somehow involved in this mess."

"You really don't think they weren't?" Elliot asked, moving to sit at the counter. "I mean, there's no way they were able to get someone on the inside of that operation without being behind the entire thing. You're born into the Mad Dawgs," he said, rolling his eyes at the name. "They don't accept newbies. Only blood."

"Okay, so if they were working together, why didn't they kill her?" I asked.

"That's exactly my question," Elliot scoffed. "And I'd like to have a very frank conversation with Scarlet about that."

"You really think she was in on it?" Seb asked, clearly outraged. His entire neck and face turned bright red instantly. I took a deep breath. It was like dealing with children.

"I'm just exploring all the options," Elliot told him, smiling at the reaction he got. Always the fucking shit stirrer lately. It was like he and Sebastian had traded spots. "As you both should be. Honestly, I expected you both to have that same question. The fact that you didn't makes me worry that her pussy has wiped your brains."

"I'm going on a fucking walk," Sebastian said, storming out of the room. A few seconds later, the front door slammed. I sighed and turned my attention back to Elliot.

"I get it. I get why you're suspicious of her. But I'm hoping leaving you two here to work out your demons will bring you back to your senses, El. She's here to stay. She wasn't a part of her own torture, and she sure as shit isn't a mole."

"Whatever you say, captain." He gave a mock salute and turned to leave.

"Elliot," I said, making him pause. "Don't kill each

other, and make sure you actually hear her out when you're having this…discussion. Okay?" Another salute and he was out of the kitchen, probably headed off to the gym in the garage.

I downed my coffee, wishing we had thought to stock this place with alcohol before we left it last time. Caffeine just wasn't going to cut it for much longer. I needed something stronger to get through the constant bickering.

God, I really hoped leaving Elliot here with Scarlet wasn't going to come back to bite me in the ass.

CHAPTER
eleven

TRISTAN

I knocked softly on Scar's door, not wanting to scare her if she was sound asleep. I couldn't imagine how exhausted she must have been after weeks of not sleeping in a bed. But since Seb was out walking god knows where and Elliot definitely wasn't going to keep her company, I was more than happy to take care of her for a while. It had also been a few hours since she had eaten, and she needed to eat again to take her meds.

"Yeah?" Her soft voice came from the other side of the door.

"Hey, princess," I said, walking into the dimly lit room and closing the door behind me. "I brought you some water and a little lunch. You need to eat so that you can take your meds again."

"Thank you," she said, trying to prop herself up.

"I'll help you, hold on." I walked over to the bed and sat down the water and soup on the nightstand. Picking her up was like lifting a small child. There was no meat on her. They couldn't have fed her a single thing in the couple of weeks she was with them. There was no other way she could have lost so much weight so fast. I placed her in a sitting position and made sure there were enough pillows to support her back and ribs.

I handed her the water, and she smiled up at me before taking a sip. She started in on the soup and groaned as she took the first few bites.

"I never thought I would be so happy to eat chicken noodle soup," she said with a laugh. Fuck, I had missed her laugh something fierce. It made my chest swell when I heard it and saw her eyes light up just a bit.

"How're you feeling?" I asked her in between bites.

"Still in a lot of pain," she said, sitting the soup on her lap and leaning her head back. She looked and sounded utterly exhausted. "Mentally and physically," she admitted. I reached out and took her hand in mine.

"You've left Thing One and Thing Two alone together down there?" she asked, changing the subject. I laughed and nodded to her to resume eating. I wanted to feed her every morsel of food in the entire house just to see her get some meat back on her bones.

"Sebastian needed to cool off, so he took a walk. I think Elliot is working out, but I honestly couldn't tell you. I haven't really been keeping tabs on him. He does his own thing."

"Since when?" Scarlet asked incredulously. "You keep tabs on everyone all the time, Tristan."

"I didn't keep track of you."

She looked at me for a moment before setting her bowl on the stand next to her. I wanted to shove it back in her hands and watch her lick the bowl clean, but I could see she was determined to say what she wanted to say, and I knew better than to fight her on it.

"You couldn't have possibly known that they were trying to get you out of that house just to take me. None of us thought they even knew where we were." She had a good point. We still hadn't been able to figure out how they knew where we were keeping her, and that was another reason why Elliot thought she was behind it all.

"But I should have taken better precautions against it." The truth was, we all felt responsible for what happened to her, even Elliot. I knew him well enough to know where his anger was coming from. He wasn't fooling me, even if he was fooling Seb and Scarlet. I knew he felt guilty, and he was taking it out on everyone around him. "It's all my fault, Scar," I confessed.

"What do you mean? How is it all your fault?"

"Because I wasn't there for you. Because I forced Seb to leave you alone that night. He fought me on it. He didn't want to leave—he thought it was reckless—and it turned out that it was. It was a stupid decision, all for the sake of appearances. It's *my* fault, Scar." I choked back the emotions that were threatening to overflow. "It's my fault we almost lost you."

"Tristan," she said while trying to lean forward to

grab me. She flinched and grabbed her sides. "Come over here so that I don't puncture a lung trying to get to you."

I moved to her side and gently pulled her into me, holding her as tightly as I dared. I would never get the sight of her in that basement, being thrown onto the hard floor and spat at, out of my brain. That image was scarred in my brain for the rest of my life, and it all happened because of me.

"I was more worried about our image that night than I was about you," I told her. "I thought you would be fine with the rest of the guys there. I never anticipated them coming in full force like that. I'm not trying to make excuses for my actions—I just hope you'll forgive me one day for leaving you like that. I'll never do it again."

"There isn't anything to forgive, Tristan," she said, drawing patterns with her fingers on my arms. "I need you guys to stop blaming yourselves." Her icy blue eyes met mine, and it was relieving to see some of the spark back in them that had been missing last night. "I'm not that easy to get rid of."

"Thank god for that," I said, laughing and stroking her hair. "How're you feeling with some food in you? Want to take a shower before we change your bandages or just go ahead and sleep for the rest of the afternoon?"

"Feeling better, even though I'm still tired. I feel like I'll never be awake again," she said through a yawn. "But a bath sounds nice. Could you run me one?"

I kissed her forehead and helped her sit back

against the headboard before getting up to get her bath ready. I looked back at the soup on the nightstand.

"Eat the rest of your soup and drink the rest of your water while I get it ready for you, okay? We need to build your strength back up if you're going to be our badass woman again, yeah?"

"Yes, mother," she joked, picking up the rest of her food and making a show of eating it before I disappeared into the adjoining bathroom.

Once the bath was full, I went back to get her and found her sound asleep, hunched over awkwardly with the empty bowl in her hand. I smiled to myself and moved it, picking her up gently from the bed. She sighed and laid her head on my shoulder but didn't wake up. Having her back in my arms, even though she was more fragile than before, sent all the blood rushing straight to my cock.

The way her ass had turned red under my belt not that long ago still played on repeat in my head, like my own personal porno. Her moans, her sighs, the way she tasted…fuck.

Fucking focus.

I was half-dressed in now-tented sweats, and she was in Seb's old shirt, but I didn't want to just lay her limply in a bath full of hot water, and I didn't want to wake her to undress her. So I just stepped in with her and sunk us both into the bubbly water up to our chests and cradled her back against me.

She moaned and rolled her face into my neck.

"What's this?" she asked, moving her hips so that her ass rubbed against my very stiff dick.

"You've already had enough play for today, Scarlet," I said, laughing as she bit my jawline. Her hands moved to my waistband and tried to work my sweats off my hips. "Scarlet," I said in a warning tone.

"If you don't lift your fucking ass so that I can pull these off of you and slip you inside of me, I'm going to get myself off and just make you watch."

I groaned at the thought of having to watch as she rubbed herself, her sweet cunt gripping her fingers instead of my dick. No way in hell I was going to let that happen. I quickly lifted my hips, making water slosh over the rim of the tub, as her laughter filled the small room. I let her slide my cock free before gently lifting her a bit to line me up with her slit.

She grabbed me and held me in place as I slipped inside of her slowly, both of us groaning together. She was so hot and wet and tight that I almost lost control and came on the spot. Her pussy gripped my dick like she was born to have me inside of her.

I took a few deep breaths and then began to move my hips in slow circles. The water splashed around us and over the bath, making a mess I couldn't care about. I gave her clit attention with one hand and rolled one of her nipples with the other. She gasped and let her head fall back on my shoulder. I still remembered every spot she liked to be touched and the rhythm she needed to get off. Her cunt squeezed me with each little thrust inside of her until she was moaning my name and digging her nails into my arms.

"You're close, baby girl," I said as I kissed her hair. "Let go for me." Her moans turned into the sweetest whimpers as she worked her hips as much as she could against me, taking what she needed from me.

Heat spread through my body as I got close to losing it as well. My brain went cloudy, and it was all I could do to hold on and not grip her and rut myself into her until she screamed out in pain.

"Yes, Tristan," she moaned as her pussy pulsed around my cock, setting off my own orgasm. I felt myself spill into her, electricity sparking through my entire body as I emptied myself into her. We both moaned and twitched together as we came down from our high.

"I swear I didn't come in here to fuck you," I said after I had caught my breath. She just laughed.

"You guys are all treating me like a porcelain doll. I'm still the girl I was when you first met me. I'm just a little bruised. It doesn't mean I don't want orgasms." I laughed and kissed her hair.

"Why don't you let me wash you off in the shower now? I don't think you want to wash your hair in cum-contaminated bathwater." I soaked up her laughter like a sponge as I slipped free of her and carried her to the shower. Before we even finished, she was sound asleep once again in my arms, clinging to me like I'd disappear in her sleep.

Never again.

CHAPTER
twelve

ELLIOT

I watched as a pack of kids pushed and chanted mean shit at the scrawny kid with the blond hair I had seen around school. He just stood there and took it, letting them call him stupid, unimaginative names and push him around the circle. A final hard shove sent him falling to the ground, his pack that he was holding to his chest colliding with his face.

"Hey," I said, shoving off the brick wall of the school and making my way over to them. They all turned their heads towards me, including the kid on the ground, who looked more terrified of me than he did of the ones actually bullying him.

Not that I could blame him. I was only fourteen and already bigger than any other kid in our class. Having a father that ran a very organized drug ring made you toughen up as a kid, and quick. I had to make sure I was able to take on a fully grown adult by the age of ten in case any of dad's business partners went rogue.

"What's up, Phan?" one of the guys asked as they saw me approach. They all backed up, letting the blond kid stand up and collect himself.

"Leave him alone," I said to them and nodded my head, letting them know it was time for them to leave. They scattered like roaches.

"Didn't ask for your help, mate," he said as he swung his pack over his shoulder.

"You're new here. Tristan, right?"

"Yeah, just transferred," he said, looking around nervously.

"Foster system?" I asked. His eyes swiveled back to me and narrowed.

"What do you want?"

"Why don't you come home with me? Mom is making a big dinner because we have family visiting, so there would be more than enough." He looked up at me, and I could tell he was wary and confused as to why I was being nice to him. There was something in the way he looked at each of those guys, like he was plotting his revenge, that got to me. There was a calculated evil in his eyes that my dad would go nuts for.

"Why?" he asked me.

"Because you are in desperate need of real food, and I need someone to talk to that isn't over forty. Come on," I said, nudging his arm. "Let's go. You can call your foster parents when we get to mine, and then we can take you home after dinner."

He sighed and looked like he wanted to bolt, but he followed me anyway. I held a small amount of guilt for bringing someone into the mess that was my family. They'd welcome him with open arms once they saw the type of person he was capable of being *deep down. Dad was going to make that shit come to the surface kicking and screaming.*

"Elliot," Tristan said, knocking me back to the present as he came out of Scarlet's room. I looked up at him. His hair was still wet, and he had a towel wrapped around his waist. What was it with him and Seb that they thought she couldn't fucking bathe herself?

Jealous? I pushed that thought out of my head and rolled my eyes at him.

"Get your turn in?" I asked him, pushing off the wall and following him down the hall to his room.

"What did you want, El?" he asked in an irritated tone. Everyone was irritated with me lately, and I couldn't blame them. I was irritated with myself. I knew that I was acting like an out-of-control moody teenager, but I couldn't help myself. My anger was on full blast ever since she had been taken. And now that she was back, it didn't seem to help anything. Part of me wanted her gone, and the other part of me wanted to go in there, carry her to my room, and tie her up, screwing her until she blacked out.

I wanted my fucking turn.

"When do you two leave?"

He disappeared into his closet as I leaned against his doorway.

"We hadn't really gotten that far in the discussion," he answered. "But I think we need to leave sooner rather than later."

"You think Seb is going to be okay leaving her so soon?"

"At this point, it doesn't really matter. We need to get back there and get our ducks in a row before we lose control. Are you going to be able to keep her alive while we're gone?" he asked as he walked back out of his closet, his lower half thankfully dressed.

"I just want to have a talk with her." I shrugged. I wanted to have a talk with her, and I wanted to get the truth out. I needed to believe her if this was ever going to work between all four of us.

"You know if we come back and you've hurt her, Seb will probably try to kill you." He paused. "I don't think I'd stop him." That stupid all-knowing smirk was back on his face, and he seemed so relaxed compared to the Tristan of the past weeks.

"Let him try. I need to go through my own process to trust her. You know this."

"I've experienced it," he said, shooting me a death glare before pulling a sweater over his head. "Remember, she isn't at full strength yet. She can barely walk from the bed to the toilet without help. There's no way she could survive what your family put me through."

"I'm not my father," I growled. I may have used a lot of the tactics my dad taught me growing up, but I wasn't anywhere near as unhinged as he was. The shit he did to me and Tristan to teach us *lessons* was beyond sadistic.

"You might not be him, but you are a trained interrogator, and even though I think Scarlet could maybe handle it at her best, she definitely can't at her worst."

"Is that an order, oh fearless leader?" He rolled his eyes at me again. I wasn't sure when I had decided to become this person—the grumpy kid that everyone had to put up with because they couldn't get rid of them. I'm sure they were wondering the same thing.

"You know what? It is." He moved closer to me, getting in my face and training his into a calm anger. I had seen him use that exact face so many times on Seb and the other guys, but he'd never had to use it on me. "Do not give her any more trauma than she already has. Have your conversation with her. Get your answers you seem to need, and then leave her alone."

I scoffed and moved to leave his room, but he called my name before I could escape.

"I'm serious, mate. I know I've known you longer—you're like a damn brother to me—but I'm not fucking around when I tell you not to become your father. You need to learn to trust your instincts. I know deep down, you trust her and you want to be a part of this, but your dad has wormed his way in so deeply, you can't let go. Seb and I need you to let it go. Scarlet needs you to let it go."

I grabbed hold of the door and slammed it shut, not caring if it woke their precious princess. Fuck, I needed to get my shit under control. He was right—my dad had royally fucked me up when it came to trusting people. The shit he put me through as a kid and into adulthood to train me had made me hard, physically and mentally. He was a master at beating the trust out of me on a weekly basis. I was always confused as to how it hadn't affected Tristan in the same way.

As I passed Scarlet's room, I could hear her snoring coming through the door, and it scraped over my skin like nails on a chalkboard. I was torn between wanting to shove a sock in her mouth to shut her up…or my dick. She had a very unique talent of being able to piss me off at the same time that she turned me on. Opting for the safest option, I punched the door as I walked past, but it did nothing to settle my blood.

Maybe Seb's idea of taking a walk in the bitter cold wasn't such a bad one after all.

CHAPTER
thirteen

SEBASTIAN

I didn't know how I did it, but I convinced Tristan to let us stay and make sure Scarlet was recovering for a few days before we took off back to London. Neither one of us let her out of our sight for long. She acted like the fussing over her was smothering and would push us away every once in a while with a laugh, but we could all see through it.

Her eyes didn't have the same mischievous glow behind them anymore. She was struggling with her demons, and neither one of us wanted to leave her to struggle alone. Almost every night, even if one of us was with her, she would wake up screaming and, on occasion, try to beat the living shit out of us.

"Seb?" she asked as she rolled over and threw a leg over my waist.

"Pet?" I answered her, turning to look at her soft face. Even in just the week we'd had her back, she'd started to look healthier. I was thankful I was able to convince Tristan to let us stay the extra days, but today had come more quickly than I thought it would. I had barely been able to sleep. I lay in bed, listening to the sound of her breathing and hoping the sun wouldn't rise. I didn't want to leave her in Elliot's *care*.

"Were you planning on saying goodbye?" she asked as she rolled on top of me slowly, pushing herself further under the covers. She disappeared under them with a smile, and her hot mouth left a trail of kisses from one side of my hips to the other, biting the skin hard enough to leave marks. My cock instantly took notice of where she was going and sprung to attention.

"Scarlet," I groaned as she dug her nails into my thighs and teased her tongue up my shaft, bringing it fully to life.

"Hm?" she moaned as her lips wrapped around my head. The suction, the heat, and the little ball of her piercing was heaven, but when she sank down completely and I felt the constricting muscles of her throat, I almost exploded on the spot.

"Scarlet!" I warned, grabbing her by the hair and pulling her demon mouth off my cock. She smiled up at me before trying to force herself back down. "Alright, pet," I said as I pulled her up and draped her over my body. She laughed and then took my mouth in a violent kiss.

"Can't handle a blow job, my little cinnamon roll?" she said in between kisses along my jaw.

"Please don't use the word *little* right now," I groaned as she gripped my dick and teased her slit with the head. My hips had a mind of their own and began lifting with each pass she made across her wet heat.

"Aw, Seb," she cooed, stroking me and sending hot shocks through my spine. "Are you about to come undone for me?"

"Enough." I gripped her waist and flipped her onto her back, sliding inside of her at the same time. Her back arched, and the most beautiful gasp fell out of her open mouth. Those icy blue eyes rolled and closed as she ground her hips against mine.

"Fucking finally," she moaned, clawing her nails down my back and then gripping my ass. The bite of her nails brought me back down to Earth as I started to move inside of her. "Stop treating me like I'm broken, and fuck me, Sebastian."

Who was I to deny my little pet?

Propping both of her ankles on my shoulders, I kissed the inside of her calf before rutting into her like a man possessed. My thumb circled her clit, and I watched her tits bounce with each thrust inside her. She positioned her hands on the headboard, holding herself in place while I tried to fuck her into the mattress.

I pushed both her legs off me, slipping free of her and leaning over her to grab a pillow before shoving it under her hips, giving me a better angle. She closed her eyes with a gasp as I pushed back inside of her. I watched as she began rubbing her clit and squeezing a nipple, working her body just the way she liked. There was nothing hotter to me than watching her touch herself, taking what she needed.

"Keep hitting that spot," she said between each thrust I gave her.

"Look at me," I told her. Her breathing became shallow, and her eyes opened and locked with mine.

"There's my girl," I said. "Let me see how pretty you are when you come."

She let out a little whimper, and then I felt her cunt around my cock, ripping my own orgasm from my body. I fell forward with a shout, crushing and grinding our bodies together as we came, her arms and legs wrapping around me and holding our sweaty bodies together. Our breaths mixed as we pressed our foreheads together, coming back into ourselves.

"Thank you," she whispered.

"For the orgasm?" I asked, playfully kissing the tip of her nose. "You're welcome." I flopped to the side of her, panting like I had just run a marathon.

"Seb," she laughed. "Shut up. No, I meant thank you for not treating me like I can't handle anything physically or mentally anymore. You and Tristan have got to stop babying me, or we'll never get back to normal."

I looked over at her, taking in her pale skin, still discolored with green and yellow fading bruises, and felt my stomach turn. I had seen enough bruises and cuts on myself and others to last me a lifetime. Over the years, I had become almost immune to seeing death and destruction around me. It was a part of life. But every day that I saw them on Scar's body, it sent me spiraling.

"That! That look right there!" she said in an exasperated tone as she stood up from the bed. "That's what I'm tired of seeing every time you guys look at me! Get the fuck over it! I'm healing. I'll be fine, and I can handle Grumpy while you're gone."

She swung open my bedroom door, stark fucking naked with my cum dripping down her thighs, and walked down the hallway to her room, slamming the door. I pressed the heels of my hands into my eyes until I saw sparks. She was right. We really needed to stop treating her like glass, but knowing I was about to leave her here with Elliot had me on edge.

"Trouble in paradise, brother?" Elliot asked, leaning against my doorframe. He was doing that a lot lately, showing up when he wasn't needed or wanted.

"Why're you lurking around the house at this hour?" Everything he did lately annoyed the shit out of me. Now with us leaving Scarlet alone with him while we went to London made him fucking unbearable.

"Heard the commotion. Thought I might check it out, see if the bitch had finally turned and tried to kill you."

I could hear the smugness in his voice, so when I finally turned my head to look at him, it didn't surprise me to see him smirking. I was really tempted to get my naked ass up and knee him again for calling her a bitch, but he wasn't worth the expended effort. So instead, I flipped him off.

"Mature," he said. "I'm going to the garage to get a

workout in before you guys take off. If you want a little brushup on your skills before you leave, let me know. Could probably use it."

"You're lucky I'm exhausted postorgasm, or I would get out of this bed and beat your ass while I'm still naked, and that would just be so embarrassing for you."

He scoffed and walked off as I went back to vigorously rubbing the shit out of my eyes. We were going to leave in a few hours, and there was no way I was going back to sleep knowing I'd pissed Scarlet off. So instead, I made myself get up and get dressed to take Elliot up on his offer. Maybe throwing punches at his pretty face would help me get out of my head.

CHAPTER
fourteen

SCARLET

I watched Tristan and Seb drive away from the front window. I could feel Elliot standing behind me, watching my every move. The silence in the house was palpable. The further away they got, the thicker the tension grew between us. I felt him lurking behind me, his gaze as heavy as the damn house we were in. It was crushing me.

"What now, Grumpy?" I asked once the car was out of sight. I turned around and faced him. He had a smirk on his face that went straight to my pussy. It was a look that promised violence, and after the week of pampering I had received from Seb and Tristan, I needed what Elliot could give me.

"You have them wrapped so tightly around your

little finger, you know that, Scarlet?" He began to slowly advance on me. With every step he took towards me, I took a step back. "Was that your plan all along? To infiltrate us? Get on our good side? Make us weak?" He took a step towards me with each question until we became a crude version of ring-around-the-rosy.

"Oh," I said when it all clicked in my brain. "You think I'm a mole." He smiled and took a few more steps towards me. When I took another step back, I ran into a wall. He advanced on me quickly, grabbing me by the neck and crushing my windpipe.

"Poor little mouse, caught in a trap," he said, his face inches away from my own. He smelled like toothpaste and bodywash. His hair was still wet from his shower and hung down over his face and into mine as he leaned closer. "We're going to have some fun today, Scarlet. Just the two of us."

"Promises, promises," I wheezed, smiling right back. He had to have known I got off on the violence. He had watched me come after stabbing someone to death, for Christ's sake. The thought of a little torture from Elliot already had me soaked. As he squeezed my throat tighter, I moaned at the heat spreading through my body.

He glanced down and watched me make a show out of rubbing my thighs together. His eyes skimmed back up my body, taking in every piece of me. I was only wearing one of Seb's shirts and a pair of Tristan's boxers. They both liked to see me in their clothes, and I didn't like to play favorites. His eyes finally met mine, and they mirrored my heat. I knew his was from anger, but I could still see the desire lurking under the surface. I just had to pull it out.

"I should've known after the stunt at the warehouse that this shit would get you off, princess. But this isn't about pleasure," he said, gripping my throat even harder and lifting me up the wall and off the floor. "This is about getting some fucking answers."

I moved my hands to his wrist, trying to get him to loosen his hold. A shiver of real fear made its way down my spine when I realized how truly alone we were and how angry he actually was. I was still healing from the multiple beatings I'd taken, and I had barely gained any strength back. The look in his eyes told me he didn't care.

Even though I was scared of what he could do to me, I also desired it. I craved it. I needed him to know that I could handle him and his demons. I could take whatever it was he needed to throw at me. And once that shit was done, maybe he could finally move past whatever it was he was holding against me and fuck me already.

"Well?" I asked after he had stood there holding me up by the neck and staring into my eyes for a long moment. My voice came out as a rasp, but it got the point across.

His free hand swung up to collide with my face. Since I was held in place by my neck, I couldn't look away to lessen the blow. The entire side of my face lit up like a Christmas tree. The sting made my eyes water, and I could almost taste blood. Instead of showing him that it had hurt, I just looked into those dark eyes and smiled.

"That all you got, precious?"

His face turned red, and I could tell he could barely see me through the rage flooding his veins. With little regard to my still-healing ribs, he grunted as he threw me over his shoulder, making me wince. I gulped down air and then smacked his ass as he carried me off in the direction of the garage.

"Knock it off," he growled.

"Are you taking me to the garage? Doesn't that seem a little careless? Won't the neighbors hear? There's got to be horrible insulation in there compared to the bedrooms."

"I don't want to get blood on the carpet," he answered. "And you'll be gagged."

"How do you expect to get answers if I'm gagged? I feel like you really haven't thought this through, pal."

"Do you ever shut the fuck up?"

"I know a way you can make me," I countered. He groaned and slammed the door shut to the garage after we entered. I couldn't really see anything other than Elliot's ass. Not that I was complaining with those buns of steel. The man was a beefcake. He worked hard for that ass, and it deserved to be bitten. I laughed at the thought and pressed myself forward, opening my mouth and grabbing a chunk of his bum in my mouth and biting hard. He was wearing gym shorts, so it was easy to get a good hold on him.

"Bitch!" he shouted and smacked my ass hard enough to leave a mark. I cried out in shock before he dropped me down onto the floor like I was a sack of potatoes. My ribs did not like that, and tears welled up in my eyes before I could stop them. I didn't want him to see me as weak. He needed to know I could take it without falling apart.

"What's first on the torture agenda?" I asked, trying to discreetly hold my ribs as I sat up.

There were storage shelves along one of the walls filled with black plastic tubs with yellow lids. He walked over to them and started pulling them down, opening them and searching for the one he wanted. When he finally found it, a sadistic grin formed across his lips. That little smirk had me clenching.

Fuck, he was sexy when he wanted to hurt me.

"Sit," he commanded when he sat a folding chair next to me.

"Please?" I chided. "Jesus, did no one teach you manners?"

"I'm about to show you the type of manners I was taught as a kid, Scarlet. For the love of God, just shut the fuck up, be a good girl, and sit on that fucking chair."

"Anything to be your good girl," I teased as I climbed up off the floor and onto the metal folding chair. "Hopefully you don't have an electroplay kink because this metal chair would be the perfect conductor."

"Oh my *god*, Scarlet," he said as he stalked over to

me. "Shut the fuck *up*." He grabbed my jaw, forcing it open, and shoved an old rag into my mouth before ripping off a piece of duct tape with his teeth and placing it over my lips.

Well, this is annoying, I thought to myself as he made his way behind me to tape my wrists together. Next, he tightly taped my ankles to the chair's legs. There was something about being restrained and spread open with broken ribs and still-healing stitches that made a girl feel a little vulnerable.

"That's better," he said, making a show of stretching and popping his knuckles before pulling another chair to sit on in front of me. "This is how things are going to work, little one." He pushed the hair that had fallen into my face over my shoulders and then leaned back in his chair. "I am going to ask you questions. They'll be simple yes or no questions, like a lie detector test."

Okay, I thought. *Does he not realize polygraphs are only eighty to ninety percent accurate?*

"They'll be easy at first," he continues. "I'll ask you questions I know the answer to, and then we'll escalate until we get to the questions I need answers for, okay? Oh, and every time you answer a question and I think you're lying? There will be punishment."

I tried to put all of the anger I was feeling into the look I was giving him. He could not be fucking serious. How was I supposed to convince him I wasn't a mole if he wouldn't even let me talk? He met my angry eyes and smiled. Fuck, it was annoying how hot he looked when he had death in his eyes.

He pulled his hair out of his face and into a messy bun on top of his head before settling in and leaning forward, folding his hands together in a falsely patient gesture.

"Let's begin."

CHAPTER
fifteen

ELLIOT

My cock was throbbing.

All of the blood had rushed straight out of my head and down to my dick. She looked helpless. Pissed, but helpless nonetheless, tied up to the chair with duct tape. It was so peaceful and quiet with her mouth gagged and taped shut. Her eyes were trained on my every movement, and all I could do was smile and hope that she was too pissed to see just how excited I was by it all.

"Is your name Scarlet Dulca?" I asked her.

Her eyes narrowed, and then she nodded.

"Good girl."

She grunted and rolled her eyes, but I saw the way her thighs were rubbing together earlier. I knew this kind of shit turned her on. Her cunt was completely open to me since I had taped her ankles to the legs of the chair, and there was a wet spot right in the center of whoever's boxers she was wearing.

I took a deep breath and tried not to let the scent of her arousal sidetrack me. It was quickly filling up the small space between us, and if I didn't get control of myself, I'd end up fucking her instead of getting answers. I realized I had been staring between her legs when she cleared her throat. When I looked back at her face, I could see that she had counted that as a point in her favor.

I slapped her…hard. Her groan sent a bolt of heat through my cock, causing it to leak into the waistband of my shorts. This was far different from any of the other interviews I'd had to do over the years.

"Is your hair black?" I asked her.

She sighed through her nose but nodded.

"Have you had sex with Seb?"

Her eyes turned up in a smile as she shook her head.

"Wrong," I said as I slapped her again. "Now is not the time to fuck around with me, Scarlet." Her cry was muffled through her gag, and when she looked back at me, a small trickle of blood came out of her nose. She shook her head to try and get her hair out of her face. I could tell by the look in her eyes she was screaming to get out of those bindings and attack.

"Have you had sex with Tristan?"

Slowly, she looked me up and down before raising an eyebrow and shaking her head again. The bitch was really going to push my limits as far as they could go.

"Fine." I grabbed her waist and squeezed hard enough to make her scream. I didn't let my hands go near her broken ribs—I didn't need to puncture a lung—but it was close enough to hurt like a motherfucker. Tears streamed down her face, and her breath was struggling to make it in and out of her nose.

"I'm not messing around here, Scarlet," I said with a harder squeeze. "This isn't a game." She screamed again, and her whole body tried to double over on itself. I let go of her abdomen and watched her tears fall. "You want to make this harder on yourself? Fine. Let's make it harder."

She looked up at me, and for the first time, the sass was gone. All I could see was fear and pain. She moaned something and continued to struggle to catch her breath. I wouldn't let her die, but I wasn't about to take that gag out and hear her incessant yammering. If she would just calm down, she'd be able to breathe perfectly fine.

"Are you a plant?" I asked as I walked over to the black box and pulled out a baton. I gave it a hard flick to extend it and watched her eyes widen as she realized I actually intended to really hurt her.

She shook her head violently.

I hummed and sat back down in the chair in front of her.

"That didn't seem too convincing." I smacked the baton across her thighs, and her whole body jerked, scooting the chair a few inches. She grunted and looked at me with hard eyes, rimmed red from crying. "Let me ask again. Are you a plant?"

She took a moment to stare at me before moving her head slowly from left to right. I took in her body language; besides the clear physical pain she was in, she didn't have any telltale signs of lying.

"Did you tell your family where we were keeping you?"

Another slow shake.

I reached forward and ripped the tape away from her mouth. She spat out the rag and stared at me, silently waiting for me to make the next move. Her blue eyes were narrowed on me, blood dripping from her nose and a bruise forming on her cheekbone. She had never looked more beautiful. I ran the tip of the baton from one thigh to another, and my cock twitched when she flinched as it went over where I had hit her before.

"Do it," she said. I stopped and looked up at her. "Do it. Beat me to a pulp, Elliot. I can see that's what you want to do, what you need to do. You need to ask me questions, but you won't believe me until I'm thoroughly beaten and broken, right?"

I reared back and gave her thighs another smack with the baton. Without her mouth gagged, she screamed bloody murder and almost tipped the entire chair over. I glanced down between her legs and saw the wet spot on her boxers had grown. I ran the tip of the baton over her pussy, and she moaned, shuffling her hips.

"What a sadistic little girl you are, Scarlet," I said as I smacked her legs again, her crying music to my ears. "I can see that wet spot growing and growing. You're drenched from the pain, baby girl." Another smack across her thighs, and she screamed again. "Are you working for your fucking family, Scarlet?"

"No!" she yelled. "I am not working for the man who tried to have me killed, Elliot! I didn't even want to be here, or did you forget? *You* all came to find *me*. *You* kidnapped *me*. I didn't just show up on your doorstep begging for a place to stay."

"How did they find you, then?"

"I don't fucking know. It wasn't my house. I was a prisoner there. I didn't even have a phone! Still don't! How the hell was I supposed to get in touch with them to let them know where I was?"

"You could have easily gotten in touch with them that day when Tristan took you into the city," I countered. "If Mel had left you alone at any time, you could've used any of the computers or phones at your disposal to call home and rat."

"And say what? Oh, hey, father that tried to kill me. Haven't spoken to you in a while, but the Triad has me, and I was wondering if you'd like to take me back in for information on them? Also, while we're at it, we should probably have me kidnapped and beaten to shit to make it look more realistic. Elliot—" She took a pause. —"I have nothing to gain here. There's no way after meeting my father you could ever think I would want to go back there."

The sincerity in her eyes during her little outburst caught me off guard. I hadn't seen this side of her. I wasn't sure if she had let her walls drop for Seb and Tristan and that's why they were so quick to trust her. But looking at her now, I could see all the pain and anxiety. She was so open and bare to me at that moment.

"You guys are all I have, now. I care about each of you. Even though you've put me through hell, I would still risk my life for you. Don't you think they begged me for information while they had me? I was beaten. I was starved. They were waiting for me to break, but I didn't. You guys are my family now, my home."

Her eyes were red, and tears were streaming down over her cheeks. The bruise on her cheekbone was blossoming and growing, causing her eye to swell. The welts on her thighs were also turning purple and blue. Her entire body was shaking with pain and desire.

I leaned over and ripped the duct tape from her ankles and then walked behind her, doing the same with the tape around her wrists. I grabbed the back of her neck and forced her to stand up. She whimpered as I turned her around and pulled her closer to my body. Her hips instinctively pushed towards my own, causing her soft belly to rub against my aching cock. I groaned and pushed back.

"If you are lying to me, Scarlet," I said, lowering my face to hers. "If you hurt either of my brothers, I will flay you alive. Do you understand me?"

I kept a hold of her neck, forcing her head back so that she had to look me in the eyes. Her tears had stopped, but her pupils were blown wide, almost eclipsing her icy irises. She licked her lips and pushed against my cock again.

"Understood," she said, her voice breathy and dripping with sex. I pulled up on her neck, lifting her body onto her toes as I leaned closer.

"I'll trust you for now, little one."

"Now who's the one that won't shut up?"

Before I could start another fight, our lips smashed together in a storm of lust and anger. I could taste the salt of her tears as she opened up to me, our tongues sweeping into each other's mouths. My hands dropped to her ass, and she jumped into my arms, wrapping her legs around my waist.

"Finally," she moaned into my mouth as I carried her off to my bedroom. Little did she know, my tastes in the bedroom didn't venture far from my tastes in torture.

CHAPTER
sixteen

SCARLET

He tasted like anger. Every movement his body made was an act of war. He carried me upstairs to his bedroom, devouring my mouth and my moans the entire way. I could feel the very tip of him press against my clit each time I rolled my hips against him. When we finally reached his room, he tossed me down onto his bed.

"Stay."

I gave a mock salute and watched him dig through his closet before he found what he wanted: rope. A lot of rope. As he unraveled it, I looked around his room for the first time. I had never been allowed in his room. I got a brief glimpse of his bedroom on the loft tour, and I had ventured into his room once at the manor house before getting caught and promptly thrown out on my ass.

This room was different from the other two I had seen. It was more Elliot. Everything was dark and moody, plain and simply decorated. But the bed frame was a different story. It was made of solid wood, jutting up nearly to the ceiling, and had thick beams connecting the sides.

"Eyes on me, little one," Elliot said, bringing my attention back to him. He was untying the endless amount of rope that was a bright shade of red.

"Kinky," I said, smiling up at him. "I've always thought red was my color."

"I've been practicing Shibari for a long time, Scarlet. I know how to tie you up in pretty little knots that you'll never be able to get out of. I know how to tie you up and suspend you in the air without hurting your ribs, and at the same time, keeping your legs spread wide open for me."

The smile he was giving me spread a violent heat through my body. I was flushed and needy for him. I wanted his hands on me. I didn't think I would be able to survive feeling him touch me with each pass of the rope. My nerves were already frayed. I was bleeding and bruised, and so horny I probably could've come just from his breath on my clit. And he was about to make me wait even longer.

He advanced on me, giving me a look that told me to stay still before his hands ripped Tristan's boxers violently off my body. I groaned at the burn of the fabric against my skin.

"Those were Tristan's favorite pair," I told him.

"He'll get over it," he answered. His hands gently positioned my legs where he wanted them, bringing my ankles to my ass. I was soaked and open for him, but he didn't linger. He began to slowly make loop after loop, starting on my right leg, making sure I couldn't straighten it, before moving on to my left. Each pass of his fingertips on my skin sent shivers down my spine.

When he was finally done with my legs, he ran his hands over the knots and watched as gooseflesh broke out across my skin. A deep growl came from his chest before he grabbed Seb's shirt and ripped it away from my body as well. He took another line of rope and began to tie my arms and chest. He crossed my arms under my breasts, pushing them out obscenely, and began to tie over my chest and down around my waist, making sure none of the ropes touched my broken ribs.

With each knot he tied, his hands flexed, and a little concentrated grunt would escape his throat, sending tingles down my spine. I could feel my wetness dripping down onto the sheets below me. God, how I hoped he would punish me for making a mess. His hands were works of art as he looped and tied the red rope around my pale skin. They were scraped and calloused from his endless workouts, and I wanted to feel them move over my skin.

My breathing was coming faster as my anxiety sparked to life. I wasn't sure if I trusted that it wasn't actually going to be agony for me, hanging in midair in the condition I was in. There was also the question of whether or not this was always his plan—to get us alone, tie me up, and torture and kill me. When he was done having his way with me, was he sadistic enough to just end it there?

Lost in my own thoughts, I didn't realize he was beginning to lift my body until my hips weren't touching the bed. He had lost his shirt somewhere in the process, and I watched as his muscles rippled with each pull. Grabbing the other piece of rope, he began to pull both through the beams at the same time, effectively lifting my entire body into the air.

There was a small amount of discomfort with my ribs, but it wasn't anything I couldn't handle. The pressure from the ropes suspending my body and the light scratching against my oversensitized skin was enough to take my focus off my ribs. I also figured once Elliot finally decided to touch me, it wouldn't matter how much pain I was in; he would distract me from it completely.

"Elliot," I said, watching him tie me off and step away from the bed.

"Sir," he said in a stern voice, meeting my eyes for the first time since he had begun tying me up. "In this bedroom, Scarlet, when we are playing—" He paused and ran his palms up my shins and down my thighs, stopping right before he got where I wanted him. "—you will call me sir. Understood?"

A thrill ran through me, and I let my head drop back, my black hair fanning out on the bed below.

"Yes, sir."

"Good girl," he said, and then his thumbs were

pushing me open to him, spreading me wide. He was so close I could feel the heat of his breath fan across my clit. My body moved on its own, trying to get closer, but all it did was make the rope scratch against my heated flesh, making me needier.

"Please," I whined, lifting my head to look at him. Our eyes met, and he smiled.

"I knew your pussy would be so pink and pretty for me, Scarlet. You're so wet," he murmured, looking back down and inspecting me. "Look at you. That tight little hole is already pulsing and begging for something to grip onto. Should I give it what it wants?"

"Yes please, sir," I whimpered, my head falling back. I tried to suck in air to calm my racing heart, but the moment his mouth descended on my pussy, I lost all coherent thought. His tongue drove into my needy cunt as his teeth scraped across my clit before he moved up and sucked. A low, guttural growl came out of my mouth as I tried my hardest to move against him.

"You taste like my own little slice of heaven, Scar," I thought he said. He was so deep inside of me it came out muffled.

"Shut up and let me come."

He was suddenly gone, and in his place was a hard slap across my wet slit, making the sting so much worse than it needed to be.

"Elliot!"

Another slap.

"You don't call me Elliot, and you definitely don't tell me what to do. This isn't going to be a loving fuck like you get with Tristan or the playful kind you get with Seb. This is me and you, working out our demons on each other. Surrender to me, empty that pretty little head of yours, and just feel. Let me take care of you."

When I didn't answer, he took it as silent consent and got back to work. As his mouth worked magic, he pushed one finger inside of me, causing my back to arch and push me into him. He growled, and the vibration sent shivers across every nerve in my body. His free hand reached underneath my body and latched onto my hair, pulling my head back. That little bit of pain mixed with the intense pleasure his mouth was causing, it was an onslaught of sensations.

"Ask before you come," he said, never stopping the perfect rhythm inside of me.

"Please…I—I need to. Please, sir. Please let me come. I'm going to come. I need it." I was a babbling mess, the pleasure rocketing through my body and effectively turning my brain into mush.

"Okay, Scarlet," he laughed. "Come so prettily for me, baby."

As he sucked my clit into his mouth, pulsing his tongue on it like a goddamn vibrator, I came. I screamed, and my entire body went tense, and he just kept pushing and pushing inside of me, making me ride each and every wave that overcame me.

"Stop, stop, stop," I begged as he continued to suck and nibble on my clit. It was too much. It was becoming painful, and I couldn't take it anymore. He gave me one last hard suck that had me screaming and my belly tensing before his mouth left me with a pop.

I panted and lifted my head to look at him. His lips

were shining with my release as he brought his finger to his mouth and sucked it clean, all while holding eye contact with me. My head dropped back again, my muscles too exhausted to hold it up.

"That was a fun start," he said. "Now let the real show begin."

How the fuck was I going to survive him?

CHAPTER
seventeen

ELLIOT

Finally getting to be the one to make her scream was the closest I'd ever gotten to a spiritual experience. As she hung there, breathing heavily against the ropes, I watched her tight little body come back down from the high of her orgasm. My dick was throbbing and begging me to push inside of her, but I wanted to have some fun first.

The smell of her on my lips was intoxicating, making me want to lie down and lower her sweet body onto my face and make a feast out of her all day. I wanted her to beg me to stop until she passed out from pleasure.

Instead, I went back into my closet and dug through the other toys I had stashed away in there from when I used to live here full-time. After my parents passed, I didn't want to stay in their home. So I moved into this safe house as a way to separate myself as I processed what the fuck I was going to do next with my life. Tristan had eventually found me and convinced me to come back to the city.

But in the time I was living here, I had accumulated quite the plethora of toys, and I had never bothered getting rid of them. I always thought I might as well have at least a few at each place, in case we ended up having to stay there for any length of time. It's not like I was sleeping around every time we had to move locations, but I wasn't celibate.

"What are you doing?" I heard her ask. She was dead tired; I could tell by her voice that she was about to fall asleep. That would change once I started playing again. I finally found the vibrating anal plug I wanted to use on her and hoped it was still somewhat charged.

"I'm going to play with you a little more," I told her as I walked back over to the bed. She followed me with her eyes until I stood behind her, my dick at her eye level. Her gaze stuck there for a moment before looking to see what I was holding in my hand. I brought it up to her mouth and rested it against her lips.

"Suck," I told her as I pushed it into her mouth. She made eye contact with me as her tongue swirled around the soft silicone of the plug. Her lips closed around it, and I felt the pull of her sucking as she took it completely in her mouth. My dick was leaking and throbbing with every pull of her mouth and swirl of her tongue. I couldn't wait to shove my dick into her hot mouth.

"Enough," I said, pulling it out of her mouth before I thought I would lose my willpower and fuck her right there. She grinned and watched me walk back around and settle between her thighs.

Using two fingers, I gently spread her pretty pink lips open, exposing her wet slit as I blew cool air over it. She gasped and flexed her hips, trying to get closer to my mouth. I ran the plug over her clit and then dipped it into her wet hole, fucking her slowly. When she was moaning and writhing, I pulled it free. She groaned at the denial of her second orgasm.

"I thought you begged me to stop earlier?" I asked her while pushing the tip of the plug into her ass. She tensed up, and I landed a hard smack on her cheek. "Relax. It's going in whether you do or don't, so…" I trailed off and watched as her body reluctantly released the tension.

I pressed harder, watching her slowly let it disappear inside of her tight hole. Seeing her relax and stretch for me sent waves of pleasure through my body. I let it slip back out a little and then pushed it further in. Back and forth, I fucked her with the little toy until it was completely sheathed inside of her and her cunt was dripping its juices down onto the toy.

And then I turned it on.

A low moan made its way past her lips, and I smiled as I watched her pussy and ass pulse around the vibrations. Gibberish flowed from her lips in whispers while I traced circles around her clit with my fingertip.

"Please, please, please," she chanted in whispers. Just as I felt she was about to fall over the edge, I stopped and slapped her clit. She cried out and swung her head up to give me a dirty look. I slapped it again. When she opened her mouth to complain, I slapped it again.

Her head fell back, and she moaned. She got off on the pain just as much as she did the pleasure.

"I want you to come just from the plug and me slapping your dripping cunt." I slapped her again, and she jumped at the contact but moaned, trying to move in the ropes and push her body forward.

"Yes, sir," she answered. Her immediate acceptance of my control was almost too much of a turn-on. If I didn't get my shit under control, I was going to blow my load in my shorts.

I alternated the intensity and the speed of her spanking, going light and quick for a while before I would really let one crack against her a few times. Her lips were swollen and red, slick with her juices that my mouth was begging to taste again.

"I want to hear your screams again, Scarlet," I told her as I picked up the speed. "Be a good girl and come for me, sweetheart."

Her breath caught, and her body tensed as she arched her back, and I watched her pussy pulse and her ass grip around the plug. She cried out through her orgasm, chanting "yes" over and over again. I stopped spanking her, giving her abused little clit a much-needed break.

While she recovered, I pulled down my shorts and then my boxers, letting them fall to the floor and stepping out of them. My cock stood proudly out from my body, begging for one of her holes. I fisted it and gave it a few strokes before lining it up with her pussy.

"Yes, please," she whined, trying to grind down on the head of my cock. "Please, sir. Please fuck me." Her voice took on a whole new tone. She was whimpering and needy, a moaning mess. I loved when strong women put their bodies and their pleasure in the hands of another person, recognizing the power in being truly submissive. She looked so sweet as she hung there to be used however I saw fit.

"You want my cock, Scarlet?" She lifted her head and nodded, looking like she was on the verge of tears. "Use your words, baby doll."

"Yes, please, sir."

I pushed inside of her, slowly, not wanting to rush and miss a moment of being inside of her for the first time. It was a tight fit, even with how wet she was. I moved in carefully, fitting an inch inside of her at a time. Between the tight grip of her and the vibrations coming from her ass, it took a lot of control to not come on the first stroke.

"Fuck, you're so big," she said breathlessly.

"Take it," I told her and pushed in to the hilt, my balls pressing up against the vibrating end of the plug. My abs contracted, and I gripped onto her hips, talking myself off the ledge.

"Jesus Christ," I moaned as she adjusted to my size. Once she started grinding her hips, I began to thrust against her. Her body swung against me with each thrust as I moved and impaled her on my cock over and over again.

"P—please, may I come?" she stuttered, and her eyes rolled to the back of her head as she fought the orgasm. I watched her struggle as I pushed into her harder and deeper, my thumb finding her clit and torturing her even more. "Please!" she shouted.

"Yes, baby. Come." I laughed and kept the same rhythm, watching her come again. God, she was beautiful when she was blissed-out. Her entire body was flushed, and a sheen of sweat coated every surface of her skin. Gooseflesh broke out as her orgasm rocketed through her. Her pussy squeezed me, begging for me to fill her up with my own release. I held out and waited for her to come down before slipping free of her. Scarlet's entire body was limp and breathless.

"Open up, baby," I told her as I made my way back to her face. "I want you to see how heavenly you taste."

She lazily opened her mouth, and I pushed the head of my cock inside of her hot mouth. She instantly sucked me further in. Losing all control as she sucked me harder and harder inside of her throat, I began fucking her mouth like it was her cunt. I watched her chest heaved as she gagged on it. Drool slipped from the sides of her mouth, and her throat bulged with each thrust inside it.

"Your throat is so fucking tight for me, baby," I praised her as my balls slapped against her face. She moaned when I praised her, and it sent me over the edge. I let myself go. I spilled into her throat, holding it there as the orgasm washed over me, sending shot after shot of cum deep inside her.

I pulled out of her once I was done, and she took

gasping breaths between coughing. I leaned over her and kissed her hard, tasting the salty mixture of our releases on her tongue. She pushed hard into my mouth, silently begging for contact. I threaded my hands through her hair and peppered kisses along her jaw and up over her cheeks where her tears had fallen.

"Good girl," I told her as we took a moment to look at each other. "You're ours."

CHAPTER
eighteen

TRISTAN

"Who is he?" Sebastian asked the guys that stood around us. Three of our top men were pulled into the meeting to try and figure out where we went from the situation we found ourselves in. And who the hell could try and help us hold our ground while we were busy protecting Scarlet at the safe house.

"Some family member, not sure," Niko answered in his Irish lilt. He was the youngest of the group, but he had proven himself useful in the last few weeks. "He's been seen a lot out and about with her da."

"So, he's being groomed, then," I said aloud, but mostly to myself. "Is this the reason they wanted her out? Because they had someone else in mind?"

"They would've had to have had men in mind from the start. That's how families like that work," Niko said.

"My family back in Ireland runs the same type of shit. Women get trivial businesses to look over while the men are actually in charge. Either that or they get shipped off to marry someone all in the name of a truce." He threw his cigarette on the ground and stomped it out. "It would never be someone random though," he continued. "Gotsta be a family member or someone that's been around long enough to be trusted. Rule number one: never trust anyone outside the family."

"So you think it's been going on for a while?" Seb asked.

"Based on us observing how friendly they are with each other and our intel, yeah," Finn answered. "Simon here has been tracking them," he said, nodding towards the guy dressed in all black like he was some undercover spy. Although, considering he used to be a high-ranking official in the American military, he might very well have been.

"Simon, how close are we on finding out who he is?" I asked, turning my attention towards the older man with a shaved head.

"It's taking a while. Their family lineage is a pain in the ass to get through. They've got everything locked down like they're the damn Tsar of Russia."

"There hasn't been a tsar in, like, a hundred years, Simon," Finn told him, laughing when the old man shot him a glare that could have even made me want to back down.

"You know what I mean, you little shit," Simon spat at him.

"How long?" I asked him again.

"A week. Maybe less."

"Let's make it less," Seb said, his patience running a bit thinner than mine was. He was anxious to get back to Scarlet. We both were, but I had been used to putting my feelings aside for the business for a lot longer than he had. I was always the one that had to turn it off for the better of everyone else. Seb had never quite mastered that.

Simon nodded and walked off, probably off to his lair in the basement, where he hid away most days.

"You got a picture of him?" I asked Niko.

"Yeah, I can send the files over to you in an email. If we're right and they are grooming him to take over, they've definitely been doing it for a while. So he's been around. Maybe show him to your old lady and see if she recognizes him. That would help Simon."

Sebastian burst out laughing, doubled over and wiping tears away from his eyes. When Niko looked from him to me, confused and worried he had done something wrong, I started laughing as well.

"Never, ever," Sebastian said between laughs. "Never, ever let Scarlet hear you call her that. She would castrate you."

Niko's eyes went wide, and Finn joined in, laughing and giving Niko a slap on the shoulder.

"And they'd let her," he told Niko as his phone rang. "I've got to take this, lads. If you guys need anything else, I'll be around."

We waved him off and made sure we got the email from Niko before sending him off as well. The pictures showed a guy that looked to be around our age, and he was most definitely a member of the family. The resemblance to Scarlet was indisputable. He had cropped black hair, and their skin tone and even the way they held themselves was the same.

"Jesus," Seb breathed, looking over my shoulder. "They could be twins."

"So, she definitely knows him. That's a family member, and you don't live your whole life in a family like that without knowing every extended relative you have."

"Unless they hid him," Seb mumbled.

"What do you mean?" I asked, shoving my phone back into my pocket.

"I dunno." He shrugged. "I wouldn't put it past her dad to hide him from her, make her feel like she was the important one, make her feel safe. If you think about it, would she have felt safe from them if she knew there was someone waiting in the wings to take her place?"

"I honestly have no idea how these fucked-up families function, so I don't know." I dropped my head back and cracked my neck. "We need to go check on the Tower and make sure everything is in line there without Mel before we can go back."

"We need to have a proper memorial for her." His irritation leaked into his voice, but I didn't know what the hell he wanted me to do. He wanted to stay with Scarlet; he wanted to protect her and keep her safe. It wasn't like we could have a memorial for Melody at the same time, letting Scarlet out into the public eye for any available sharpshooter to take a shot out.

"We will, Seb," I told him, placing a hand on his shoulder and squeezing. "We will. Once this shit settles down and Scarlet can be out and about, we will do it immediately."

"While we're here," he drawled out in a singsong voice, "we need to pick up Scarlet's Christmas present."

"We haven't got her any presents yet. We haven't even had time to talk about it, let alone think about it these last few weeks. What did you get her?"

"Okay, don't be mad at me."

I sighed and pinched my nose. If he was asking for forgiveness before telling me what he did, I knew it was going to be fucking huge.

"Bear in mind, please, Sebastian, that we brought the Maserati and not a Boeing 757. What the fuck did you get her?"

He just looked at me and smiled, that panty-dropping smile that made even me think he was handsome. He only used it when he really wanted to get away with something. Anxiety created a black hole in my stomach.

"Not a what." He paused for dramatic effect.

"What?" I finally asked.

"Not a what," he said again, placing both of his hands on my shoulders and leaning in. "But a *who*."

CHAPTER
nineteen

SCARLET

"I was thinking," I told Elliot as he sat on the floor in the bathroom while I showered. Turned out, he wasn't the "let me wash your hair" type. He was amazing at aftercare. He had brought me all my favorite foods, held me while I drifted off to sleep, and massaged the sore parts of my body that were scratched by the rope. But washing my hair? Big fat *no*.

"Yes, Scarlet?" he asked.

I looked at him through the frosted glass. He was just sitting on the floor, his back against the wall and his legs outstretched and crossed at the ankles. He had an iPad in his hands, scrolling through something in his email. It had been a few days since Tristan and Seb left, and the house was eerily quiet without them, especially since Elliot wasn't the chattiest of the group. He followed me everywhere like a hulking, silent shadow.

"I think we should make them a big dinner for when they get back."

"Neither of us can cook," he said in a bored tone.

"We can try," I told him as I turned off the water and wrung out my hair. It was getting too long, but there was no way in hell any of these oafs were going to cut it. "I think it would be nice!" He handed me a towel through the door, his eyes never leaving his iPad. He was acting more and more like Tristan every day.

"Oi!" I said, plopping my wet self down on his thighs in between him and the tablet. "Pay attention to me." I grabbed his face in my hands, and he smirked.

"I am paying attention to you. It's called multitasking." He leaned forward and kissed me, his mouth dominating mine as I opened to him. "If you want to have a nice family dinner," he said as he trailed kisses across my face and down my neck, "then we should just order it in."

"And pretend we cooked it?"

"They'll never believe that," he said with a laugh as his hands gripped and kneaded my ass. We were having sex multiple times a day, fucking like teenage kids without their parents around for a long weekend. My pussy was sore and needed a damn break. I pushed his hands away and stood up, wrapping and twisting my hair up into the towel.

"Fine. As long as I get to pick where we order in from."

"As if you'd let it happen any other way," he said, picking the tablet back up and scrolling.

"Any news?" I asked hesitantly. I knew he wanted to wait until they were home to go over everything together, but I wanted to be involved when it was my life on the line.

"They've seen someone hanging around your dad a lot," he said, locking the screen and looking up at me. I hopped up on the bathroom vanity and started my skincare routine.

"Okay," I drawled. "That's not unusual. He always has people around him, and we knew he would have to find someone eventually to take his place. He's probably grooming someone."

"They said he looks like a family member, early twenties. Short black hair, looks a lot like you, supposedly."

"I mean, I have a few cousins around my age that look like me. Our family genes run strong, believe it or not," I said with an eye roll. "Romanian blood through and through."

"Anyone you can think of that would be close enough to him for him to have been grooming him since he was a kid though? Isn't that how families like yours normally work? It's what my dad did, training me since I could walk to know my place."

A little bit of sadness flitted across his face before his mask settled back in place. *Poor Elliot*, I thought to myself. He was always fighting some internal struggle. He always felt like he needed to look like the tough one.

"I had a cousin I was really close to growing up," I

said, remembering how we used to play together as children. "His name was Motshan. He was just a few years older than me, I think. I'm not sure. My father told me he was taken to Romania to be with family when I was about ten or so. But," I said, hopping off the counter, "if it is Motshan, we're in luck."

"And why's that?"

"We were close. He was like a brother to me, my best friend. If my father has decided that he should be the one to lead, he'll be on our side. He'll leave us, and more specifically *me*, alone."

I smiled, thinking back to all the days we had together. I didn't really have any friends growing up. I wasn't allowed to attend normal school like all the other kids my age. I was homeschooled by a governess, keeping me locked away and virginal for whoever they decided to marry me off to later in life. That hadn't really worked in their favor.

But Motshan and I, we got to be kids together. We ran around outside, played hide and seek in my family's manor home, and went swimming in the lake. I told him all my secrets, and he told me all of his. We were inseparable. After my father told me his family had taken him back to Romania, I was crushed. I was a ten-year-old kid getting her best friend ripped away. We didn't even get to say goodbye.

I shoved my toothbrush into my mouth and started scrubbing vigorously.

"That's assuming your family hasn't gotten their claws in him."

I looked at Elliot in the mirror. He was staring up at

me with open and honest eyes. He wasn't saying it to be hurtful; he was just saying it because it was something he was worried about and he wanted to share that with me. It was taking a while to get used to this side of him. The side of him that wanted to tell me things just to talk and volley ideas back and forth, instead of the side that said things to hurt and poke.

"I really don't think he could be corrupted," I said after I spat. "Mots and I were best friends, and we both hated the life we had to grow up in. If anything, he'll be dreading the takeover. But maybe he can actually do some good in the family."

"Sources say they're pretty close, acting very friendly with one another."

I smiled down at his worried face and outstretched my arms. He grabbed my hands and lifted himself off the floor, colliding with my body gently and pulling me into his arms. His hair was pulled up in a messy knot on the top of his head, accentuating all of his sharp features and almond eyes. He was so beautiful when he wasn't scowling that it almost took my breath away.

"He'll be an ally," I told him as he grabbed under my ass and picked me up. My legs instinctively wrapped around his waist. "And I would actually love to see him, to maybe set up a meeting one day."

"I'd like to stop talking about other men now," he said, grinding his hips against my center. My forehead dropped to his shoulder, and I nibbled at his neck.

"I'm sore," I told him in a whiny voice as he turned around and pressed my back against the wall. "And I just showered."

He pushed down his sweats, and the hot length of his dick sprang free and pressed against me. I was already wet, and the head of him slipped in easily. I gasped and bit down on the crook of his neck.

"So wet, little one," he purred, his breath hot on my ear. "I know you're sore, baby girl," he said as he took my hair out of the towel and fisted it. He slid in slowly but easily. I felt incredibly stretched by him every single time. He touched nerves inside of me that I didn't even think existed. I was panting, and my hips were rotating, trying to fit him the rest of the way in. "But you can take it."

With that, he rammed himself inside of me, sheathing himself to the hilt. My scream was loud and brutal as he pulled my hair back, letting my neck fall open for his mouth. He pumped inside of me with ruthless abandon, grunting and moaning like a man possessed. I loved him this way. I loved seeing him unravel right in front of my eyes.

I reached down between us and played with my clit, pushing myself closer and closer to the edge.

"Good girl," he cooed, looking down between us and watching us fit together over and over again. "God, you're perfect," he moaned.

His constant praise lit me up. It was such a change from how he normally treated me that it was all the more special. Heat grew and spread through my belly and spine, making my toes curl.

"Ask," he ordered.

"Please?"

He held my eyes with his for a moment, changing

his angle and hitting a whole new spot. My mouth fell open, and my mind went blank. I could barely breathe as he rutted into me.

"Come."

It was like a gunshot, a lightning bolt of shock through my body. My muscles contracted and released, fluttering and gripping his cock. He kept up his pace but hit that spot inside me harder, making me cry out his name as wave after wave of the orgasm rushed through me.

I was a rag doll pinned between him and the wall, there to be used and fucked as he wished, and I loved every minute of it.

He cried out my name as his own orgasm rushed through his body. I could feel him inside of me, his cock jerking and spilling into me, painting my insides and claiming me as his. He smacked my ass as he came down, both of us panting and sweaty.

"Now I need another shower."

He smiled and kissed me, his lips soft against my own.

"I'll help you," he said with a wink. My insides flipped at the promises that look gave.

CHAPTER
twenty

SEBASTIAN

"Okay, when you said we were going to get Scar's old roommate for her Christmas present, I just assumed you meant you had discussed it with her."

I looked over at T and gave him a confused look.

"Where's the fun in that?"

"Seb," he sighed as he shook his head. "We can't just break in to Kenna's home and take her!"

"Why not?" I asked. "We just took Scarlet."

We were sitting in our car outside Kenna's apartment building. In my defense, I thought doing things this way made a lot more sense. I'd had her vetted by the boys, and she was clean. She had absolutely no ties to anyone we needed to worry about. She was just some girl in London. And if we just walked in and took her, it prevented anyone from finding out we planned to take her to Scarlet, therefore eliminating any other issues that might pop up.

"Scarlet was different."

"Scarlet *is* different," I agreed. "Anyway, let's get this over with. I want to get home to my girl."

"Our girl," he growled. I rolled my eyes at him. In my opinion, he hadn't done much yet to earn her back, but whatever. If Scarlet was happy to have him back, I would let it go.

We both got out of the car and made our way into the apartment building. It really was far too easy to get into the place, and the stairwell smelled like stale piss. It made my stomach turn to think of my Scarlet living in a place like this. Thank god we had kidnapped her.

Once we made it to her door, I reared back to kick it open, but Tristan stopped me.

"You really think Scarlet is going to be okay with this? Kidnapping Kenna and scaring the shit out of her? Also, kicking down her door seems a bit extreme."

"We'll pay to have it fixed," I pouted. I wanted the dramatics of a good surprise, so before he could actually stop me, I swung my booted foot and kicked it in. I heard Kenna scream from somewhere inside and smiled at Tristan's pissed-off face. "You're so cute when you're pissy," I told him, pinching his cheek before stepping into the flat.

"What the fuck do you two want?" Kenna all but screamed as we both stepped into her living room. It was a dingy thing, poorly lit with a sofa and a chair that had definitely seen better days. Kenna was sitting on the sofa, a bowl of cereal in her hands and the TV playing some trashy reality show. "Where's Scarlet?"

"Excuse Sebastian and his flair for the dramatic," Tristan said, stepping around me and taking in the living room. Kenna sat her bowl down onto the coffee table and gave us both appraising looks.

"Where's Man Bun?" she asked.

"Babysitting." I shrugged.

"We thought maybe you'd like to see Scarlet?" T asked her. Her eyes went wide for a moment before she recovered. I could tell she was gearing up for a fight. Those brown eyes of hers sparked up just like Scarlet's did before she tried to rip me a new one for something stupid I did.

"Yeah, this isn't up for debate," I said before stalking over to her, grabbing her around the hips, and throwing her over my shoulder. She let out another scream and started punching my ass. "You leave a bruise and you'll have Scar to answer to," I told her. "She's very fond of my ass."

"Sebastian," Tristan warned. I laughed and held her tightly behind her knees as she continued her assault. He sighed and pointed towards the door. "Get her down to the car before she makes a scene. I'll grab some shit from her room."

"See what you did?" I asked her as we made our way down the stairs. "You went and pissed him off. Now we're going to have to sit in the car with grumpy Tristan for the next few hours."

"What the actual fuck is happening right now?" she

asked. She gave up her fight as I crossed the road to the blacked-out Maserati.

"You are going to be Scarlet's surprise Christmas present!" I told her excitedly. I couldn't wait to get her back to the safe house and surprise Scarlet. I hoped she cried. She was always so fucking pretty with tears falling over her cheeks.

"Good to know Scarlet is still alive," she deadpanned as I tossed her into the back seat. "Nice car," she said, running her hands over the soft leather seats. I clicked on the child's lock and shut the door and then did the same on the other side before sliding into the passenger seat. "Scarlet isn't, like, chained up in your basement like a dog, is she?"

"Kenna," I said as I turned around to face her. "I'm appalled you would think so little of us." She snorted and rolled her eyes, looking out the window and watching T cross the road with a bag packed full of her stuff. He opened the back door and set it on the seat next to her.

"Sorry," he said before shutting the door and climbing into the driver's seat.

"What are you sorry for?" I asked him.

"I'm apologizing to Kenna because *you* just kicked down her fucking door, and *you* fireman carried her out of her flat. We just kidnapped her. If we had done it like normal people, we would've contacted her first and asked her if she would like to visit Scarlet as a surprise." His stern look stayed trained on me for a minute before he started the car.

"Not really on brand for you guys to do things the right way," Kenna chimed in from the back seat.

"See?" I said to Tristan. "Even Kenna agrees this was the correct way to do it."

"I didn't say that," she said.

"No one asked you, Kenna Kardashian."

"Don't call me that," she said as she kicked the back of my seat.

"Don't kick my fucking car seats!" Tristan said, slapping her feet off the leather. "I just had this car detailed. I'd appreciate it staying clean for longer than two fucking days!" Kenna started murmuring to herself, and I turned back around in my seat.

"Will you please drive us back to our girl now?" I asked as I buckled myself up.

"Oh, she's our girl again?" he asked with a raised eyebrow.

"Until you fuck up again. Then she goes back to just being mine."

Kenna, surprisingly, was quiet in the back as we drove off towards the safe house. If she wondered about our relationship with Scarlet, she didn't say anything. Maybe she was waiting to talk to Scarlet herself. I couldn't wait to get back to her. I was missing her scent, her taste, and her moans. We had only been gone a few days, but I was addicted to her and going into serious withdrawals.

Elliot wasn't very forthcoming about their time together, but he had told us they were getting along and had gotten past whatever shit it was he was holding against her. Tristan hadn't pushed for any details and told me to leave it alone, but I wanted to hear every dirty detail there was.

I wondered if he had shown her his fun side, tying her up and fucking her while she was a helpless little thing. Did she scream for him? How pretty and gaping did her used little pussy look after he used that monster on her?

My dick started to swell at the thought, and I leaned my seat back, palming over my jeans. I couldn't wait to get back to her, feeling her perfect little cunt grip my cock and pull me in. I wanted her nipples between my teeth and my hands wrapped around her throat. I loved it when I choked her so hard she could just open her mouth in pleasure, not making a sound as her eyes rolled into the back of her head.

"What the *fuck* are you doing?" they both asked as I *really* started rubbing.

"What?" I asked, looking at both of them but not stopping. "I'm horny."

"Sebastian, lean your seat back up and think of your grandma in church or something. You are not about to rub one out in my fucking car that, once again, I just had fucking cleaned!"

"Not to mention the complete stranger in the back that really doesn't want to see you cream your pants, dude," Kenna said.

I sighed and pushed my seat back up. It made my jeans press painfully against my swollen dick and balls. I held them and tried to adjust everything so that I wouldn't have to sit in pain, and out of nowhere, Tristan swung and slapped me across my face.

"The fuck!" I said, slapping him back.

"I said stop!"

"I did stop!" I shouted. "I was adjusting!"

"God, do you guys ever shut the fuck up?" Kenna complained. "How does Scarlet deal with the constant bickering? You two fight like you're an old married couple. I can't imagine what you're like with Man Bun in the fucking mix."

I scoffed and adjusted myself one last time, then held up my hands in surrender when Tristan gave me another warning look.

"Let's just get back, yeah?" Tristan asked.

"That's what I've been saying," I mumbled to myself as I looked out the window. I heard him sigh, but otherwise, he didn't engage.

"Fucking men," Kenna sighed.

CHAPTER
twenty one

SCARLET

"They will literally never believe you made all of this," Elliot said as he walked back inside. He had taken the trash out for me, effectively hiding the evidence of take-away containers. I looked at the spread on the dining room table. I had decided on Italian. I figured it was the easiest type of food to pretend I made. How hard was it to make some pasta and sauce?

"It's pasta!" I chastised him. "They really aren't going to believe I made some fucking pasta?"

Elliot just smiled and shrugged before walking off to look out the living room windows for the guys. They were due back any moment, and I couldn't wait to get my hands on them. I was excited to have all my boys together under one roof…and possibly in my bed. That could prove to be fun.

"What're you thinking about?" Elliot asked, turning his attention back to me.

"Me? Nothing." I smiled and started pulling plates out of the cabinets. "Can you get the champagne, please?"

His arms were suddenly around my waist, pulling my ass into his hips, where I could already feel him starting to swell. Elliot was insatiable. I thought Sebastian had been the one that was going to ruin me, but Elliot took sex to a whole new level. He was ready to go any time of the day. It didn't matter if we had just gone for a round, he was more than willing to give me orgasms until he was hard again.

"You had that look on your face," he whispered in my ear before nibbling on it.

"What look?" I asked, leaning back into the solid wall of him.

"That look when you need a cock to fill one of your holes." He pressed hot, openmouthed kisses down my neck, pushing my hair out of the way to get access to more of my skin.

"I have a look for that?" I asked with a smile, tilting my head to the side, trying to give him as much access as he needed. I thought about Tristan and Seb walking in the house, catching us close together, and it sent a thrill through me. Would they watch? Would they want to join in?

"Of course you do, my little slut." He bit down hard on my shoulder, making me gasp and push my ass harder against him. I could already feel myself getting wet and excited for the promises he was whispering in my ear. "Would you like it if they walked in while I fucked you on the counter? Do you like the idea of them watching me stretch you and listening to your moans as I hit that perfect little spot inside you?"

He turned me around and lifted me by the hips, sitting me down on top of the counter as he settled between my thighs. He was so tall that he still had to bend over to level his face with mine. His eyes roamed over my face like he was creating a mental map, drinking me in and memorizing every little freckle and wrinkle.

Elliot leaned in slowly, making me anticipate his next move. I watched with anxious eyes as he got closer, his breath fanning across my mouth. His lips brushed across mine with the lightest touch, making my breath catch in my throat.

And then the front door crashed open, and I looked over to see an eager Sebastian running towards me. I laughed as he made his way over with a determined look on his face. He pushed Elliot out of the way and took his place between my thighs. His hands gripped my face.

"Hi," I said.

"Hi, baby," he said with a panty-melting smile and then kissed me like his damn life depended on it. He could've sucked my soul right out of my body he kissed me so hard. His tongue darted into my mouth, warring with mine as I fought right back. I threw my arms around his neck and pulled him as close to my body as I possibly could.

"Get a fucking room," Elliot mumbled as he sat plates out at the table.

"Set an extra place," Seb said to the side once we came up for air.

"What do you mean?" I asked him.

He leaned in and kissed my nose.

"Happy Christmas, little pet," he said and helped me down from the counter. He nodded towards the door, and I watched as Tristan walked in with someone else behind him.

No, I thought to myself. *It couldn't be.*

"Kenna?"

She walked into the house, her eyes wary. My heart soared at seeing her again. I pushed Seb out of the way, ignoring his fake sounds of protest, and ran over to her. She smiled as I took her in my arms, lifting up her small frame and letting her wrap herself around me like a koala.

"Bitch, did you send your kidnappers to bring me here? Because I really don't like the idea of being held captive."

I set her back down on her feet and grabbed her face, smushing it and looking her over.

"I missed you," I told her.

"Hey, princess," Tristan said, leaning down to kiss my cheek. "Happy Christmas."

"Hi, handsome," I said, turning and standing on my tiptoes to take his mouth in a kiss. Kenna watched us all with blatant curiosity. She had to have so many questions. I knew I would have if I were in her shoes.

"Why don't you two get food and go catch up?"

Tristan suggested. "Seb and I will tell Elliot about the trip, and we'll come see you later, okay?" He kissed the top of my head, and I smiled, taking Kenna's hand and pulling her over to the kitchen to fill our plates with food. "Can you guys help me get all the bags?" Tristan asked Seb and Elliot.

I saw them both roll their eyes, knowing it was just an excuse to give me and Kenna the room for a moment, but I was thankful. Kenna visibly relaxed once they were out the door.

"Are you fucking all of them?" she asked, her eyes wide as I filled her plate. I let out a loud cackle and leaned over to kiss her cheek.

"Oh, we have a lot to catch up on, Ken," I told her with a laugh. "We can go up to my room. They'll leave us alone." I thought for a moment. "Well, I know Elliot and Tristan will. Seb may try to join. He's a bit clingy," I said with a smile on my face. "And he's definitely going to try and get a threesome out of this." I laughed at Kenna's shocked face.

Once our plates were full, we made our way up to the room I was staying in. I cleared off the bed, and we sat down to eat. It was fucking delicious. There was no way any of them were going to think I had cooked it.

"Yeah, you definitely didn't make this," she said, shoving her mouth full. I wondered when the last time was that she had a decent meal. When we'd lived together, we pretty much survived off ramen and cereal.

"So," I said between bites. "Ask away."

"Are you fucking *all* of them?" she whispered.

"I am," I whispered back, giving her a wink. I laughed. "You don't have to whisper. They all know I'm fucking all of them. Well, I'm not sure if Elliot told them we finally slept together while they were in London, but they'll know soon if they don't know already."

"And they're okay with that? How did this happen, Scarlet? Last I saw, they were literally kidnapping you. Now you're, what, in some kind of poly relationship with them?"

I sighed and sat my fork down, trying to think of how I could explain what happened without sounding like I had completely lost my mind. Kenna didn't really know about my past. She didn't know I had grown up in a world like this. I was going to have to tell her everything to make her understand. I was going to have to start from the beginning so that she could see where I had come from.

I picked up my glass of champagne and downed the entire thing before pouring more from the bottle we had brought upstairs with us. She watched me with a worried look on her face. I took a few more gulps and then passed it over to her.

"Kenna," I started. "This shit I'm about to tell you can't…it's a lot. You can't tell anyone, okay? Not just because I'm trying to save the boys or because I'm trying to save myself. This kind of shit could get you in trouble too if the wrong people found out." I reached out and grabbed her hand. A little frown formed between her eyebrows as she nodded.

So I started at the beginning and told her everything. I told her who my family was and how they tried to have me killed. I told her how I ran away, trying to escape them and hide. I told her about the boys and how we had gone from them turning me over to me convincing them to keep me, and also how I may or may not have convinced them to do so with sex.

She listened to everything without interrupting or asking any questions. Once she was finally caught up, she just gave a small laugh and threw back her own glass of alcohol.

"I'm so incredibly jealous of all the grade A dick you're getting, dude," she finally said.

We both looked at each other for a moment before we burst out laughing.

"I'm so glad you're here," I told her after we both were able to get ourselves together.

"I am too. I missed you. But I need you to tell Nose Ring to fix my fucking door. And maybe next time, if they want me to come hang out, you can tell them they don't have to break down my door like fucking Rambo."

"Yeah, that's kind of Seb's style," I said with a smile, thinking about my murderous cinnamon roll. "But he's a sweetheart."

"Alright, then," she said, moving our empty plates off the bed. "I want all the dirty details. Who's the biggest? Who's the kinkiest? Who had the strongest head game? Spill, bitch."

I laughed and settled in for a long night.

CHAPTER
twenty two

SCARLET

I woke up with two strong bodies sandwiching me in bed. I nuzzled into the chest in front of me and inhaled the fresh, clean scent. After Kenna had gone to bed, Seb showed up first, wanting to hold me as I slept. Not two minutes later, Tristan had come in, asking to sleep with me as well. I had missed them and welcomed both of their body heat into my bed as I drifted off.

"Hey," Sebastian mumbled from behind me. "Get back here." His voice was rough with sleep as he scooted up closer behind me, pressing his morning wood into my ass.

"Too early," Tristan said, breathing in as he ran his nose through my hair. Sebastian's hand ran over my hip and around to my belly, where his fingers made little circles on my bare skin. The top I was wearing had ridden up overnight, leaving my lower half completely exposed for his wandering hands.

"That feels nice," I said into Tristan's chest. Seb's fingers dipped lower, teasing and taunting me, moving everywhere except where I wanted him to go. My breath caught with every pass lower and lower. My hands dug into Tristan's skin, using him as an anchor for my frustration.

"Too early to play with our little pet, T?" Sebastian's teeth played with the sensitive skin on my neck while Tristan's fingers teased my nipples over the soft shirt. I whimpered and rubbed my thighs together.

"Never," Tristan answered before he leaned in to kiss me. His tongue licked across my lips, begging for entry. I opened to him and let him lazily explore. My mind was going a mile a minute, wondering if this was actually going to happen, if I was actually going to be lucky enough to have both of them at once.

Sebastian's hand finally dipped to where I wanted it, grazing over my slit and finding it wet.

"Our girl is already wet for us, Tristan," he said as his fingers parted me and dipped in to circle my clit. I gasped and buried my face into Tristan's neck. I felt him chuckle as his hand moved and slid under my top instead. He rolled my nipple and pinched it, causing me to grind down on Seb's hand even harder.

"Needy little thing," Tristan said. I looked up at him and gave him my best angry eyes, but he just laughed and brought his tattooed hand from my nipples to my throat, gripping it until he cut off my air supply. My mouth dropped open as Seb dipped a finger inside of me. Tristan leaned forward and licked the inside of my mouth. A moan escaped me, and Tristan swallowed it.

"Make her come," Tristan said to Seb. He let up on my throat just long enough for me to catch my breath before he squeezed again. Seb ground his dick against my ass in time with his fingers as they moved and curled inside of me, demanding my pleasure. I felt it build and build as Tristan's free hand moved between us, rubbing my clit while Seb kept up his assault.

My mouth moved, trying to form words to tell them I was going to come, but Tristan just kept squeezing. I could feel myself close to passing out, but it only enhanced the pleasure coursing through my body, and once Tristan squeezed my clit, I was gone. He released my throat, and I gulped down air while my climax rolled through my body like a tidal wave of heat and electricity. My toes curled, and my back arched, pressing my ass into Seb and my tits into Tristan.

"I want this ass," Seb said, changing his angle so that his fingers explored from behind. He was moving them from one hole to another, smearing my release to the tight ring of my ass before slowly pushing a finger inside. The burn had me whining into Tristan's mouth as he continued to play with my oversensitive clit and push a couple of fingers inside of me. I reached down between us and palmed his dick.

I pushed frantically at the waistband of his boxers as Seb's finger became wholly seated inside of me. I needed them both naked and inside me. I had never taken two at once, but their fingers were enough to drive me mad with lust. We were a tangle of limbs while we tried to get both of them undressed.

"Get your fucking clothes off," I told Seb over my shoulder.

"Yes, ma'am," he laughed.

"I want you both," I told them as they kicked their boxers off and pumped in and out of me faster. Seb added a finger, scissoring them and stretching me.

"You are not fucking her ass without lube," Tristan told Seb in a firm voice. "Go get it."

"But…" He trailed off in a pitiful voice. "I'm naked, and you just want her alone."

"Go get her lube," he said in a stern tone.

Seb slowly pulled his fingers out of me and rolled out of bed with a groan. I watched him run around the bed, hard-on swinging, and open the door, peeking out to check if the coast was clear before bolting out of the room. I laughed, and Tristan smiled down at me before rolling on top of me and kissing me slowly. His dick was sandwiched between us, his precum dripping onto my belly as he thrust against me.

"You sure you're okay with this?" Tristan asked, his face soft and open. "You're okay with us sharing you?"

"You already share me," I said, kissing the strong column of his throat.

"You know what I mean," he said, grabbing my jaw and making me look at him.

"Yes, my love." I rolled my hips up against him and nipped his chin. "I'm very much okay with this. I'm an enthusiastic participant. I promise."

He grinned and scooped my leg up into the crook

of his arm before positioning himself at my entrance and pushing inside of me with a slow thrust. He bottomed out, and my hips rolled up, wanting the sweet stretch he gave me.

"Fuck," he whispered against my neck. He pulled out slowly and then thrust back in with enough force to make the bed knock hard against the wall. "Your tight little cunt was made for us," he said as he pulled all the way out and slammed back inside me. I saw stars with each push inside of me.

"You asshole!" Seb shouted from the doorway as Tristan gave another powerful thrust, shoving the bed against the wall with a loud thud. "You fucking started without me! That's not fair!" He kicked the door shut and ran around the bed with the little bottle of lube in his hand.

I shushed him and gave him a swat as he pushed both me and Tristan back onto our sides, causing Tristan's cock to hit a new spot. I moaned and ground into him, sending shocks of pleasure through my body at the contact with my clit.

"We have a guest," I said between a moan and a whisper. "Keep your voice down!"

"You're the ones waking the whole house up as you pound the fucking bed against the wall," he snapped back. Before I could respond, his fingers, slick with lube, were pushing into me with force.

"Fuck," I groaned as two quickly became three. He moved them inside of me, stretching me to the point where the pain turned into pleasure, making my breath come in short pulls. The burn was exquisite as Tristan kept up a slow pace inside my cunt. I was so full, I couldn't imagine how it would feel once they were both inside of me, feeling them move against each other with each thrust. The thought alone had me dizzy with anticipation. "Just do it already," I told him as Tristan rolled a nipple between his fingers.

Seb slowly pulled his fingers out of me, leaving me feeling empty without them. A moment later, I felt the slick head of his dick line up with my hole. Tristan pulled out as well, giving Seb a bit more room. Tristan's dick slid easily over my clit, up and down, turning me into a whimpering puddle of need.

"Ready, pet?" Seb asked, his breath hot on my ear as he spread my cheeks.

"Yes," I said, trying to press myself down on both of them. "Get the fuck inside of me, now, Sebastian."

"Perfect girl," Seb said and began to push inside me.

CHAPTER
twenty three

TRISTAN

It was taking every ounce of concentration and willpower I had to not slam back into her hot cunt. Waiting for Seb to slowly push his way into her ass was killing me one inch at a time. And watching her face as he went deeper and deeper was a thing of fucking beauty.

Her pupils were dilated with lust, practically taking over every bit of icy blue. She looked at me, holding my gaze as he kept stretching her open. I rolled the head of my dick over her clit, making sure even through the burn, she could feel some pleasure from it.

God, I couldn't wait to feel how fucking tight she would be with another dick inside her. My balls tightened up even at the thought. She moaned, pulling my attention back to her. I ran my knuckles over a nipple and watched her chest move in rapid breaths.

"Fuck me, Scarlet," Seb groaned against the back of her neck, where he bit her in a dominant gesture. His face was scrunched up, looking like he was in a mixture of pain and pleasure. "You're so fucking tight, baby," he said, licking the mark he had left on her skin.

She panted against me, her fingers digging into my skin while she adjusted to the stretch of him.

"Okay, baby," I said in a soft voice, pushing her leg off my waist and letting Seb take it under her knee. He lifted it high, spreading her for me. When I looked down her body and saw him settled deep inside her, a groan escaped my lips. We had shared women before, and I knew the feeling of him inside of her at the same time was going to make it difficult for me to hold my composure and not fuck her into oblivion.

"Hurry up, T," Seb said in a strained voice. "I need to move." She whimpered and adjusted herself slightly, effectively grinding herself further down onto Seb. "Jesus Christ, Scarlet," he breathed. "Try to stay still, pet."

She was so fucking wet, she was making a mess on her thighs. I pushed myself inside of her slowly, relishing in the tight, wet heat of her. Between the feel of her pussy gripping me and Seb's dick on the underside of my own, I was surprised I didn't finish in one stroke. Her face was pinched as she laid her head back against Seb.

My thumb found her clit and gently made teasing

circles around it. I could feel her body relax then, welcoming the extra stretch of my cock inside of her.

"Yes," I heard her whisper. Seb was playing with her nipples, rolling them and pinching them as I finally pushed all the way inside of her. "Fuck, this is a lot," she said, a small smile trying to play on her lips. I leaned in and kissed her soft lips.

"We're going to start moving now, okay?" Seb asked. She nodded as she reached above her to hold on to Seb's hair, her left arm tucked under my neck. Seb pulled out first, his piercing dragging along her walls, causing my dick to twitch and jump at the sensation. Fuck, I would never get used to how that shit felt.

As he pushed back inside of her, I pulled out. She moaned so deeply I could feel it vibrate through her entire body.

"Yes, my pet," Seb purred in her ear as we picked up our pace, our hands never leaving her heated skin. She was flushed red, sweaty and panting. Her eyes were closed as she tried to meet each of our thrusts, chasing her own orgasm.

With each push and pull, Seb's piercing sent a bolt of pleasure down my spine.

"Fuck," I mumbled between thrusts. "I'm not going to last long like this." Scarlet smiled and wrapped the arm that was on Seb around my waist, her hand squeezing my ass as I thrust inside her.

"Tristan," she cooed, her fingers making their way into my crease. As I pushed inside her, she used one of her fingertips to circle the rim of my ass. I groaned with the new shock of pleasure that rolled down my spine. "Do you like that?" she asked as she pushed her finger a little inside of me.

My thrusts became erratic. I lost all rhythm between the sensation of her finger, Seb's dick against my own, and her pussy gripping and clenching around me.

"I want you to come with me," I told her, pressing just a bit harder down onto her clit with each pass of my thumb. I kissed her, and her finger slipped just a bit further inside of me. "Come with me, poppet," I whispered against her mouth.

Seb pushed on her back, pressing her closer to me and changing his angle.

"Oh, fuck," I growled, pumping into her with reckless abandon. "Do you feel that, baby girl?" I asked her. "Both of us owning you? Marking you?" She moaned, and Seb and I both shoved into her with force.

"God, yes," Scarlet moaned into my neck.

"This, Scarlet," I said between breaths. "This is us ruining you for anyone else…ever. Do you hear me?" She moaned in response. "You're ours."

"Right there. Yes, fuck," she moaned. She chanted both of our names like a prayer, and then she came, crying out and biting into the tender flesh of my throat. It triggered my own orgasm, and I reached out, grabbing Seb's ass to force him further inside of her and therefore pressing harder against me. I held still as I spilled my release inside of her.

Seb rolled his hips, rubbing his piercing on the

sensitive underside of my head, making me twitch and squeeze his ass cheek with a bruising grip. We were a mixture of sweaty, writhing bodies as Seb began chasing his own orgasm. He thrust in and out of her ass like she was his own personal fuck toy.

His hands found her throat, squeezing until her face turned red from lack of oxygen. I twisted her nipples until her mouth fell open in a silent scream. Seb's pounding moved us all, forcing the bed to knock against the wall over and over again. She wasn't going to walk normally for a week the way he was pummeling into her.

"Fucking *yes*, baby," he growled as his hips stuttered. "Take me. Take all of me."

He stilled inside of her, his own orgasm taking over. He thrust inside of her a few more times, letting up on her throat before she blacked out. Her pussy fluttered around me, her final orgasm soaking both us and the sheets.

All of us breathed deeply as we came back down to Earth. Seb and I kissed every inch of her skin we could get at while she just smiled and laughed, tracing little circles over our bodies.

"If you were coming to join, you're a bit late to the party," Seb said. I looked over my shoulder and saw Elliot standing in the doorway, staring directly at Scarlet.

"Look what you've done, little one," he said with a smile. I turned back around as Scar sat up on her elbow and smiled right back at him. We slipped free of her with an obscene noise. "Come take care of it," he ordered her.

"Yes, sir," she said, her eyes lighting up with the command.

CHAPTER
twenty four

SCARLET

Seeing Elliot standing in the doorway, knowing he'd heard us all together, got my already drenched pussy dripping again. I was being as loud as I could be during the scene just to try and get him to join. Him coming in at the end and ordering me around was the next best thing. I probably should've been more concerned with the fact that Kenna was downstairs, who most definitely heard the entire thing, but I was dick drunk and couldn't help myself.

I got up on all fours, ignoring the mess that the boys and I had created on the bed, and began to crawl around them. Seb smacked me hard on the ass, and I turned around, narrowing my eyes at him as he winked before getting off the bed. I went down to my hands and knees on the floor and crawled over to Elliot, making sure to swing my hips so the boys would still have a show from the bed.

When I made it over to him, I sat back on my feet and looked up at him, waiting for him to tell me what to do next.

"I'm going to shower," Tristan said with a laugh. I heard him get off the bed and walk over towards me. "Have fun, poppet." He kissed me on top of my head before Elliot let him pass.

"You?" Elliot asked Seb.

"Oh, hell no, mate. I wouldn't miss this show for anything."

I smiled but never let my eyes leave Elliot's face. I heard the bed shift behind me, and Elliot's attention was trained back on me, holding my gaze.

"Take it out," he ordered. He was wearing low-hung plaid lounge pants that showed off the sharp cut of his vee. I trailed my fingers across the dark trail of hair under his belly button and then along the waistband of his pants. His abs jumped at the contact, and I smirked up at him.

"Stop fucking around." He gave my face a soft slap. "Do as I say and take it out."

"Yes, sir," I answered, pulling his lounge pants down over his hips. I watched as his thick cock sprung free, the slit already wet with precum. His pants fell to the floor, and he didn't even bother stepping out of them before fisting my hair and rubbing the salty head across my lips.

"Open."

I obeyed and opened my mouth, letting him rub the

tip across my tongue before he slowly pushed further and further into my mouth. I brought my hand up and cupped his balls, rolling and kneading them in the palm of my hand. He hissed through his teeth, his head falling back on the doorframe. He pushed further into my throat as I relaxed and tried not to gag around him.

"Fuck, this is hot," I heard Seb say as my nose pressed against Elliot's skin. He was bottomed out in my throat, and I couldn't help but gag around him. Drool collected in my mouth and dribbled out of the corners of my mouth.

He pulled out, letting me take a deep breath before looking down at me and shoving himself all the way back in. I heard the bed shift again behind me as I continued to suck for all I was worth. He tasted sweet and salty, and I wanted him to use my throat like the other boys had just used my other holes.

I felt Seb kneel behind me and take my hair from Elliot's grip. Elliot let Seb take control of my movements, moving my face up and down on his shaft. My sloppy sucking sounds filled the room and mingled with Elliot's groans as Seb's free hand found my oversensitive clit.

"Think you can come again, little pet?" he whispered in my ear.

He was working my mouth hard over Elliot's cock. I could feel my lips bleed as they were stretched and rubbed raw, the copper taste filling my mouth. I moaned as Seb's fingers scissored my clit.

"Fuck," Elliot cursed as I began to greedily suck

him down. The faster Seb stroked me, the needier I became. I looked up at Elliot and watched him watch me. His eyes were trained on me and the way Seb was playing with my clit.

"She's so wet," Seb said against my skin.

"Fuck her," he told Sebastian. "Tease her with one finger curled inside of her. Make her ride your hand and chase her own orgasm." Elliot's gaze fell back to me. "Ride his hand, little slut. Take what you need."

I groaned as his words sent a flood of heat through my body. Seb pushed a single finger inside of me that just barely grazed my G-spot. I began rolling my hips and bouncing up and down on his hand while I sucked Elliot in and out of my mouth. I took his balls in my mouth, licking and sucking while I moaned, trying to chase my orgasm.

Every little move I made against Seb's hand was just barely enough to get me to my own release. I could feel Elliot getting closer. His hips thrust sporadically as I took him back in my mouth. Seb's grip on my hair tightened as he forced me to take Elliot deep into my throat. He held me there as I coughed and drooled down my chest.

"You better come before I do, or you aren't allowed to come for the rest of the day," Elliot said with a sinister smile. I whimpered when Seb yanked on my hair and let me breathe. I began to grind against his palm harder and faster, matching the pace with which he worked me on and off Elliot's dick.

"You're so close, baby girl," Seb said as he licked the shell of my ear. "Let go for us."

"Be a good girl and come for us, Scarlet," Elliot said from above me. Their encouragement and praise lit me up like a light, sending jolts of pleasure through every muscle in my body. I sucked Elliot into my throat, rolling his balls again in my palm. Seb hooked his finger just right inside me, and I exploded, moaning and drooling all over Elliot's dick until I felt him tighten and spill into my mouth.

I swallowed over and over again, trying to make sure I didn't miss a drop. I clenched and shook around Seb's finger until Elliot was done and pulled free of my mouth. I fell back in Seb's arms, exhausted but on an incredible high.

"Good girl," Elliot said, leaning down to kiss me on the mouth, tasting himself on my tongue. "Get cleaned up. We have company, remember?" He pulled his pants up and left Seb and me on the floor. I laughed as my head fell back on his shoulder. He pushed my hair out of my face and turned it to his.

"I love you," he said. I felt my mouth open and close without any words coming out. He laughed and kissed me, his tongue exploring my mouth without a care in the world that I had just swallowed a load from his best friend's dick.

"Sebastian," I said, pushing him away. I tried to find the right words. Did I love him? Was that what I felt for him? When I was taken away from them, I missed them like I loved them. I missed them like I'd lost a fucking limb.

"You don't have to say anything, pet," he told me before giving me another peck on the lips. "But after I lost you once, I'm not going to censor myself just because the truth may make you a bit uncomfortable. In this business, we can't afford to tiptoe anymore. I love you. You deserve to know."

"Sebastian," I said again, trying to find a way to tell him that I did think I loved him. I just had never told anyone that before, and I didn't have the confidence to just throw it out there like he did. I knew he was right. He did deserve to know how I felt about him, but my brain wouldn't think thoughts in my post-sex haze.

"Scarlet," he said with a smile that lit up his entire face. "Stop trying to think so hard. Let's get you cleaned up. Elliot's right—we have company," he said as he stood and picked me up, a ridiculous amount of fluids leaking out from between my thighs. I groaned and squeezed my thighs together, trying to keep myself from making an even bigger mess than we had already created.

"Sex is messy," I said, trying to change the subject.

Seb laughed and looked down on the floor at the puddle I left from where I'd been kneeling and then to the bed, where there was a huge wet spot from my squirting. He looked back to me in his arms and then carried me to the shower.

"That's the mark of a job well done, Scar," he said as he put me on my feet and started the shower. "And it just means I get to clean you up." He turned around and winked one of those dark eyes at me.

He was so handsome, my little murderer. His body was cut from fucking marble, and those tattoos made my pussy clench. The way he had wrapped those strong hands around my throat while he fucked my ass was enough to fuel my wank bank for a year.

And he had fought for me when I was gone. He had killed…a lot of people to get me back. He treated me like a precious treasure, always making sure I was taken care of, my hair washed, and I was fed my favorite foods. He kept me laughing and gave me all the orgasms I could ask for.

He had stood up to Elliot for me when he suspected I was working for my family. He had my back constantly.

I looked up at him and smiled, walking into his arms. His brown eyes shone with happiness as he looked down at me. He wagged his eyebrows as his arms rested on my shoulders.

"Yeah, yeah," I said with an awkward smile. "I love you too, asshole."

CHAPTER
twenty five

SEBASTIAN

"Good morning, Ken Doll!" I said cheerily to Kenna as I made my way into the kitchen. She was sitting at the table, sipping a cup of coffee. Her cheeks got bright red the second Scarlet and I walked in.

"Is Kenna too hard for you to remember, Nose Ring?" she shot back.

I laughed and walked over to make Scarlet her coffee and cereal. She sat down with Kenna and started apologizing for this morning in a quiet voice. Kenna looked a bit uncomfortable but laughed it off anyway.

"You ready to talk about everything we learned while we were gone?" Tristan asked as he and Elliot made their way into the kitchen.

"We're going to do this in front of the girl?" Elliot

asked in his usual grumpy voice. Blow jobs could only keep a guy happy for so long, it seemed.

"Why couldn't we?" Scarlet asked.

"Because we don't know if we can trust her."

After the girls had gone upstairs last night, Elliot had confronted us about how we could bring a stranger into the house without consulting him first. Tristan quickly bowed out and let me take the brunt of his anger by blaming it all on me, but he could've said no. I might have listened.

"I had her fully vetted, El," I groaned, sitting Scar's sugary cereal and disgustingly black coffee in front of her. I picked her up and sat down, placing her on my lap. Kenna watched us out of the corner of her eye. I could tell she was skeptical of our relationship with Scarlet, but she'd come around. Or she wouldn't. I didn't really care.

"Excuse me?" Kenna asked.

"Yeah," I said, running my fingers through Scarlet's still-wet hair. "Like I would bring you here, risking the safety of the woman I love, without having multiple background checks run on you?" I saw Scarlet's neck go bright red, and I was sad I couldn't see the color stain her face with embarrassment from this angle. "You were followed for a week as well. You were completely oblivious. You should really work on that, by the way. Take better stock of your surroundings."

Scarlet turned around and whacked me on the side of the head. I just gave her a smirk and watched that cute little blush brighten her cheeks.

"Whatever. I don't like it," Elliot said, sitting down

at the table next to us. "But I'm not going to argue because I'll just be outnumbered anyway." Well, maybe a blow job could keep a guy compliant after all.

"We spoke to a few of the guys that have been watching your family," Tristan started, and he sat down with us as well. "They've seen this guy hanging around a lot," he said, turning his phone towards Scarlet. "Know him?"

"That has to be Motshan," she said, taking the phone from Tristan and zooming in on each photo, flipping through them all. "God, he's grown up," she said with a wistful tone.

"Is this good news or bad, poppet?" Tristan asked as she handed him back his phone.

"This is good." I could see the worry in everyone's faces. "Stop looking at me like that, dickheads." I laughed and wrapped my arms around her waist. I was worried too. She was being oddly trusting of some cousin she hadn't seen since she was a kid. They could've easily gotten under his skin.

"Elliot said they shipped him off to Romania?" I asked her. "They could've easily turned him against you in that time."

"One hundred percent," Elliot mumbled into his coffee. I could feel her shoot daggers at him with her eyes. Her body had stiffened up at our doubting him.

"Hey," Tristan said, reaching across the table to take her hand. Kenna's eyes followed the movement. "We are on *your* side here. We just can't go in blindly assuming that he is going to be on our side."

She nodded and pulled her hand free from his,

going back to her cereal. "Let's figure out a way to set up a meeting, then," she suggested.

"Oh, absolutely fucking not," Elliot said, slamming down his cup of coffee.

"Yeah, there's no fucking way," Tristan agreed.

"Why not?" I asked. "It would give me a good excuse to hurt those assholes if they step out of line. It's been too long since I've had blood on my hands."

"You had blood on your hands like two weeks ago, Seb," Scarlet said, turning around to give me a little smile.

"Yeah, but your family deserves it," I told her. "Remember that first night together when I told you I would let you watch me dismember the asshole that tried to rape you? Cut off his fingers knuckle by knuckle?" I slid my fingertips over hers, feeling her shiver against me. "I'd still let you watch," I whispered into her ear before nibbling on the lobe.

"Jesus," Kenna muttered. I looked over at her and winked.

"Look," Tristan started before Scarlet interrupted him.

"I'm not letting this go. We could use him. If he is still the Motshan I knew, and he still has any type of love for me, he could be an ally when he takes over...if that's what they're grooming him for. Imagine how nice it would be to have my family on your side instead of at your throats."

Tristan sighed.

"Okay, can we table it for now? Let us do some more digging. Let our guys do some more surveillance before we jump into contacting him for a meeting, yeah?"

She leaned forward over the table and held out her hand, just like she did on that first night out together.

"Deal. Shake on it," she demanded. Tristan smiled and took her hand in his.

"Deal."

They continued to talk about everything Tristan and I had learned on our trip to London, but I zoned out. I was too busy thinking about how many people I could and would kill for her. If Motshan was going to ultimately be on our side, good. If he was important to Scarlet, I'd welcome him into our little fucked-up circle.

But if he wasn't…

There were so many people to kill and so many ways to do it.

I had been working on my own little side project: trying to figure out who the fuck had attempted to rape and kill my girl. I wanted to taste his blood, fucking bathe in it as he screamed and begged for his life. I had dreamed about it every night since she told me her story.

I could flay him alive, peeling off his skin in little patches and cauterizing the wounds as I went, making sure he stayed alive. I would stop when he passed out and start back up when he came to.

Or…I could pull off all of his fingernails and toenails, one by one. Then I could chop off each appendage knuckle by knuckle. Then his hands and feet. I could cut out his tongue and watch him choke on his own blood. I didn't think that option would make him suffer long enough though. We'd have to torture him before we started. Maybe waterboarding.

"Sebastian." Scarlet's voice brought me back to the present.

"Yeah, pet?"

"Why are you hard right now?"

I just grinned and kissed her cheek. We could discuss it later.

CHAPTER
twenty six

ELLIOT

Scarlet came into the garage dressed in the tightest little shorts and sports bra I'd ever seen. I silently thanked Seb for picking out her clothing for the time we spent here. Her long, dark hair was pulled up in a tight ponytail, the ends swinging around the nape of her neck.

"How can I help you today, Scarlet?" I asked her as I continued to focus on the punching bag instead of her skimpy outfit. I didn't think Kenna would appreciate me throwing her down on the floor and fucking her in the garage, where she could pop in at any time.

"I've really started feeling better in the last week," she said. "I'd like to start working out again. There's only so much TV I can sit around and watch with Kenna. I swear we have watched Jeremy Kyle's entire backlist. I can't possibly shove more trash TV into my brain."

"Stretch," I said with a smile. "We'll go slowly starting back."

"What do you think about how quiet it's been?" she asked me as she sat down on the mat. "I'm torn between being worried about it and thanking my lucky stars they're leaving me the fuck alone."

"I don't know," I answered between punches. "The guys have been keeping an eye on them back in London. They don't really seem to be doing anything other than going to big family dinners and showing your cousin around the city. As far as the Mad Dawgs," I said, "I think they're silent because their numbers were so diminished in the time they had you. We had to have wiped them nearly completely out."

She sighed, and I looked over at her. Her face had changed. She looked like I'd just killed her puppy.

"What's wrong?"

"I'm giving myself a moment to feel sorry for myself," she said, her icy blue eyes looking up at me. "My family always did like Motshan better than me," she admitted with a sad little laugh. "My dad would always take him places as a kid and leave me behind. Motshan was invited behind closed doors when I was made to wait outside until they were done. It's the normal life of a girl in that type of family, but it still sucked to feel second best."

"And you still aren't worried that Motshan is maybe on their side and won't ultimately be on ours?" I asked her. Ever since we got confirmation from her last week that the guy they were chauffeuring around the city was her cousin, I couldn't help but worry we were trading in one problem for another.

"No," she said, shaking her head and standing up. "Motshan would always come back from those trips or come out of those rooms and tell me everything. He kept me in the loop, and he spent all of his time with me. We were best friends." She smiled.

"Even at that age, you're aware of the type of family you're being brought up in. They start grooming you pretty young. So, he knew that as a woman, I wouldn't be given the same opportunities he would, and so he would always make sure I knew what was going on. He gave me the attention the rest of my family wouldn't." She took a couple of weak swings at the punching bag, cringing a bit when they jarred her ribs.

"I have a feeling you really shouldn't be punching anything quite yet, little one," I told her, moving her attention from punching back to the mat. "Let's start small and just start building your core muscles back up. Do some easy stuff, okay?"

She looked at me and rolled her eyes but listened, sitting down on the mat and started doing hip raises.

"I'm trying not to be an asshole," I told her. "But I don't trust him, and I won't apologize for it or make excuses. I've seen enough of this shit in my life to know that people can be very easily turned…especially children."

She rolled her eyes again, but I continued on.

"If they took him to Romania at that age, they

could've *easily* been taking him there to turn him against you or train him. I don't want to be the one to shit all over your dreams of a happy reunion, but the other two aren't going to do it, even though they should be. You need to be realistic about this and ready for anything your family might throw at you."

She paused and sat up to look at me.

"I get it," she said, taking my taped-up hand and squeezing it. "I know you grew up in a shitty family with shitty parents like I did, so you're wary, and I know you're saying these things just to look out for me. But Motshan was to me what Tristan was to you. Tristan was the only other kid you could trust. He was your best friend and your brother. That's what Motshan was to me. He was there for me when no one else was."

"Yeah, but Tristan was never taken away from me by my own family without explanation," I countered.

"Okay," she said, crawling onto my lap and straddling my hips. "Enough talk." She leaned in and kissed me. She had been doing this a lot in the past week, distracting us all with sex when she wasn't getting the answers she wanted.

"Hey," I said, grabbing her throat and pushing her away from my mouth. She just grinned and licked her lips. *Little fucking minx.*

"Yes, baby?" she asked, her voice rough and heavy with sex. Her hips rolled across my own, making my cock jump to attention. I growled and flipped her body over, pinning her to the mat on her stomach with her hands behind her back.

"Is this what you wanted?" I asked her as I roughly

yanked her tight little shorts down her legs. She laughed and shook her ass in the air. "Bad girl," I said and smacked her hard across her right ass cheek, leaving a handprint. She squealed and tried to move away. I slapped her until I reached the count of ten, her ass red and hot to the touch.

The entire time, she lay there squirming and whimpering, trying to get away from me. But when I dipped my fingers into her cunt, I found her dripping and ready.

"What a little slut you are, Scarlet."

She whined and moved her hips, trying to get my fingers where she wanted them. But I pulled them away and took my cock, heavy and hot, out of my shorts. I moved her hands above her head and lifted her hips slightly as I leaned over her. Lining up with her slit, I shoved myself in, not going slowly enough for her to get accustomed to my girth. If she was going to act like a slut, I was going to treat her like one.

She cried out but pushed back against me, forcing her body to take as much of me as she could. Her pussy was heavenly in the way it gripped and sucked me in. I pressed my body into hers and left a trail of bites up her neck while giving her hard little thrusts.

"You take my dick so nicely, Scarlet," I told her before sucking and biting on the soft flesh of her throat, hoping to leave a bruise. She groaned and pushed her ass into me.

"Just fuck me already," she said in that bratty little tone of hers. I laughed darkly in her ear before sitting up on my knees, lifting her hips to follow. I pushed her face into the mat and pulled almost all the way out of her dripping cunt before slamming back in.

"Careful what you ask for, little one," I told her before doing it again and again. I thrust into her like I was punishing her, bottoming out into her cervix with each drive. I abandoned shoving her face into the mat to grip onto her hips, pulling them back to match me in my rhythm. My fingers dug into her skin in a bruising hold.

She came with my name on her lips, and I followed shortly after, holding on to her to keep myself from collapsing on top of her.

"Fuck," I said as I pulled out of her and watched my cum slowly drip out of her. "That is so sexy, Scarlet." I latched onto her, sucking her clit and my salty release into my mouth, demanding another orgasm from her. She cried out as I pushed my tongue deep into her cunt, lapping at her and cleaning her up. I moved back to her clit, sucking and nibbling until her breath caught and her body went tight.

"Enough!" she yelled, falling over on her side and smacking me in the process. "Jesus Christ, Elliot," she said with a smile. "Enough before you make me black out."

I smiled down at her and kissed my way up her stomach, across her tight sports bra, and over the pulse point on her throat. I took her mouth with mine, forcing my tongue across her own, making her taste us both together on my tongue.

"That was so fucking hot," she said, coming up for air. "I've never had a guy do that before."

"I made the batch." I shrugged. "May as well taste test." I smiled as she broke out into a fit of laughter. I kissed her again, happy to lie with her on the mat and ignore the shit going on outside the door for five more minutes.

CHAPTER
twenty seven

TRISTAN

"Simon called me this morning," I told both Sebastian and Elliot. We were in the kitchen while the girls chatted away, watching TV in the living room. "He seems to think someone followed us here, or they've figured out where we're keeping her somehow."

"Who?" Elliot asked.

"Her fucking family," I answered, running my hands over my face.

"Then why haven't they made a move?" Seb asked quietly.

"Maybe they don't want her? Maybe they're just keeping an eye on her?" I honestly had no idea, but I didn't like that they had an idea of where we were. That meant this house was no longer safe.

"Or maybe they're waiting until they can secretly

get enough manpower here to make their move," Elliot chimed in, helpful as always.

"I want to make sure that there actually is someone here before we start making plans to move her. We only have so many places off the radar to take her."

"What was Simon's reasoning? Why does he think there's someone here?" Elliot asked.

"One of their guys hasn't been seen since we were in London, and he was seen on CCTV lurking around the Tower while we were there. They were probably keeping tabs on us from the moment we set foot in the city."

"Okay," Seb said. "Let's figure out if someone is here and go from there. How do you want to do that?"

I sighed and looked through the opening into the living room. Kenna had said something, making Scarlet throw her head back in laughter. I wasn't going to lose her again. We had to do something to get this shit over with. It wasn't like we could just hide her away for the rest of her life. We had businesses to run, and she had a life to live. We were going to have to bite the bullet and end it whether we liked it or not.

"You aren't going to like it," I said, looking back at Seb. "We're going to have to lure them out of wherever the fuck they're hiding, and Scarlet is going to have to be the bait."

"Oh, hell no," Seb said immediately.

"He's right," Elliot sighed. "If they're here, they're here for her, not us. The only way to figure out if anyone is here and who they are is to use her."

Seb's face fell, and his eyes went dark. He didn't like it, but he knew he was going to be outnumbered.

"If there was any other option," I told him, "I wouldn't use her like this. I really wouldn't. But I don't know what else to do, and it's not like we're going to leave her alone. We'll be there to make sure she stays safe."

"Where is this happening?" Elliot asked while Seb sulked and stared into the living room.

"Pub in town has a Christmas party they're putting on. Figured we could go there, have a few drinks, and wait around to see if anyone makes an appearance." I snapped my fingers in front of Seb's face to get his attention. "Are you listening? I know you don't like this idea, but Scarlet needs you to pay attention and be at your best. Nut up and do it for her if you don't want to think you're doing it for me."

He rolled his eyes and took a deep breath.

"We go in loaded to our fucking teeth," he finally said.

"Agreed," Elliot said.

"Same." I leaned forward on the counter, lowering my voice another notch. "We also need to keep an eye on Kenna. If anything were to happen to her, Scarlet would never forgive any of us. And," I said, smiling to myself at the memory, "we know Scarlet can hold her own in a brawl."

Seb laughed and nodded.

"Seems strange to me that all of this is happening *after* you both allowed her supposed best friend into the safe house."

Seb and I both turned our glares on him.

"What?" he asked. "You guys really don't find it odd that we were basically fine until you both trotted off to London and brought a stranger back?"

"She isn't a stranger," Seb said. "And I had her fucking watched!" he whisper yelled.

"Are we ever going to move on from this?" I asked him.

Elliot smiled and shrugged.

"If it turns out that I'm wrong, I'll move on from it. Until then, no promises."

Seb stared him down for a moment, and I thought I was going to have to break up another fucking fight between them. It had been so smooth lately with all of us sharing her and knowing she was back safe with us. But in future, I knew there was no way I'd be letting Seb spring any big surprises on Elliot that concerned Scarlet. Ever since he crossed over to the dark side, it seemed he took more of an interest in her safety than I expected him to.

His entire demeanor had shifted in the past week. He wasn't as grumpy, he wasn't picking as many fights with her, and when he did, they were playful and normally ended in him laughing and smacking her ass.

Meanwhile, I was still trying to battle the small kernel of jealousy I felt whenever I saw either of them alone with her. We had all shared women before, but never for anything serious. It was always a night or two of shared fun, and it never went further than that.

But I was falling for Scarlet, and Seb had already told her he loved her, and she had said it back. Did she love all of us? I didn't *want* to be jealous over their relationship. We were all in this together, and she was important to all of us. And the way she treated each of us proved that we were just as important to her.

"Are we telling her?" Seb asked, bringing me out of my thoughts.

"What do you think? Should we?" I asked them both.

"I think if we don't, she's going to be one pissed-off Polly that she was left out of something. Especially after what happened the last time we left her out," Seb said. "You know, like, the whole kidnapping thing."

Elliot snorted.

"Fair point," I said. "I'll tell her. Be ready by six."

"Can't wait to get the fuck out of this house. We've spent far too much time together in this small space," Elliot said before walking off into the living room and sitting down on the couch and pulling Scarlet into his lap.

"I'm starting to think you guys can't go longer than thirty minutes without touching her," Kenna said, rolling her eyes.

"Aww, K-Shizzle," Seb said, walking over and mussing the top of Kenna's head. "I can hook you up with one of the guys if you want."

"No you fucking will not!" Scarlet yelled at him. "All those guys are walking disasters, and she does not need to be dragged into this shit."

"I'm telling the boys you said that," I told her, falling down on the couch next to them. "Finn is going to be so hurt." She gave me a look and flipped me off.

"Is he hot though?" Kenna asked, a teasing smile on her face.

"Don't, Ken," Scarlet said, holding up her hand in Kenna's direction. "Don't encourage them."

I made eye contact with her and winked.

"I'll introduce you," I told her.

Scarlet threw me a dirty look before swiftly changing the subject. But I couldn't help but notice Kenna's cheeks turning pink.

CHAPTER
twenty eight

SCARLET

Tristan had explained what was going on before Kenna and I went upstairs to get ready. I didn't like that this was happening while she was here or that we had to take her out into the line of fire, but there was no getting around it. We definitely weren't leaving her behind. This little group did not have a good track record of leaving people behind.

"Remember the last time we went out to bars together?" Kenna asked as I straightened another piece of her hair. We were taking the opportunity of getting out of the house for the first time to actually make an effort. I had been wearing the boys' clothes since I got back, and it felt nice to actually wear something that was my own for once.

"I don't want to talk about it," I said with a laugh.

"Can you even remember it?" she asked, laughing at my expense. "You got turned down by five different taxis. I thought I was going to have to carry your drunk ass home on my own."

"It's not my fault that no one would bring me fried chicken." I had walked from taxi to taxi, shouting at her and the other people around me that how dare they send me home without any fried chicken. Or so I was told, anyway. I don't remember much from that night.

"You didn't have to shout it in every taxi driver's face. That was also the night you got a cigarette burn on your nose, wasn't it?" I nodded and laughed. "How the fuck did that even happen?"

"I'm telling you, I don't remember a fucking thing. I was also supposedly jumping into random circles of people and dancing, remember? The stories about that night are wild." I combed my fingers through her hair and sat the straightener back down on the sink, flicking it off. "I remember getting home and running up the stairs to vomit." I cringed at the memory.

"Yeah, I pushed you in there and went to bed. You were a bit more coherent by that point." She stood up and walked back into the bedroom, pulling on a pair of jeans.

"I fell asleep with my face on the toilet seat and woke up when my nose touched the toilet water," I told her, shivering at the memory.

"Let's not get that out of control tonight." She laughed and walked over to pull me into a hug. "I thought you were fucking dead," she said, holding me to her in a death grip.

It took me a moment to react to her sudden show of affection. It wasn't like we had never hugged, but she was pouring a lot of emotion into it, squeezing me like she had actually lost me. I shouldn't have kept her so in the dark.

"I'm sorry, Ken," I said, wrapping my arms around her. "I shouldn't have kept so many secrets. I thought I was keeping you safe, but it just made it harder on you. I'm sorry."

She pulled back and dabbed at the few tears that had escaped, trying not to mess up her makeup. God, she was beautiful. Her brown eyes were almost black, and with her heavy eyeliner, it made her look a bit alien in the best way. I grabbed her face and gave her a quick kiss.

"I won't keep you out of the loop anymore, okay?" I told her. "Forgive me?"

"Of course I forgive you," she said with a smile.

"Are you guys about to make out right now?" Seb asked, suddenly appearing in the doorway. "Can I watch?"

"You wish, Sebby," Kenna shot back. She got sick of all of his nicknames for her pretty quickly and decided to fight back with a nickname she discovered he hated. I found it hilarious and contemplated giving her cinnamon roll to add to her arsenal but decided to wait for the right moment. Seb's face fell into a scowl, and he flipped her off as she walked past him.

"I'll go grab the rest of my stuff, and then I'll be ready to go," she said, disappearing through the door.

"You look good enough to fucking eat, little pet,"

Seb said, pulling me into his arms and grabbing my ass in a bruising grip.

"Don't threaten me with a good time," I told him as I stretched up onto my tiptoes and kissed him. "Let's go get this shit over with. How many weapons do I get?" I asked him as we made our way downstairs.

"Two pistols and a few knives," Elliot answered, coming around the corner with Kenna. "This one said she has little to no experience, so I've given her one gun and a quick rundown on how to shoot, but I'd rather her *not* have to use it." He pulled his silky hair up into a tight knot. "She'll get us all killed," he murmured grumpily.

Kenna rolled her eyes at him.

"I'm not completely helpless, and I'm definitely not going to get you killed just because I've never had the reason to shoot a gun before, asshat." She stuck her tongue out towards him and then saddled up next to me.

"Let's get this shit over with. I'm already tired at the possibility of having to deal with your family," Tristan said to me as he walked down the stairs.

"Yeah, let's maybe stop calling them *my* family since they tried to kill me," I told him as he kissed my forehead. He did look tired. I looked around at my boys, trying to see if they were all worn down. I guess playing bodyguard in a safe house for your girlfriend was kind of an around-the-clock job, especially when it took them away from London. That was definitely an extra stressor.

We needed to figure this shit out and fast.

My men looked so handsome. They had all worn tight jeans and sweaters that showed off every deliciously carved muscle they had. Elliot had let his hair down once we got inside, those soft strands falling in his face. They all sat around me and Kenna, keeping an eye on everything that was happening around us as they nursed their one whiskey each.

I leaned over to Tristan, whose strong hand was creeping further and further between my thighs.

"We could always make a quick trip to the loo," I whispered in his ear. I ran a hand through his white-blond hair and tugged a bit at the ends. "I didn't wear any panties." His fingers flexed against my thigh, and I watched his Adam's apple bob as he swallowed.

"You can't say that shit to me right now, Scarlet," he murmured against my ear. "I'm supposed to be watching for someone that may want to kill you, and you're dangling fruit in front of a starving man."

I smiled and kissed him, letting my hand wander over the growing bulge in his jeans. He groaned and turned his attention back towards the table, trying his hardest to ignore me. Kenna and Seb were bickering back and forth, and Elliot was sitting stoically in the corner of the large booth, sipping his drink and watching every person that came through the door.

"Guy sitting at the bar alone keeps looking over here even though he's trying really hard to look like he isn't," Elliot said in a low voice. Tristan leaned in like he was whispering something to me and turned his head, glancing at the guy out of the corner of his eye. He kissed me and squeezed my leg again.

"He got here not long after us, and he's been there ever since, glancing around like a creep," Seb said, leaning forward on the table. He looked right at me and gave me a wicked smile, a smile that promised evil. "Can I get him for you, pet?" he asked me.

I glanced over at Kenna to gauge her reaction to the monster that was about to come out to play. She just looked back at me and downed her drink.

"Guess that's our cue?" she asked me.

I looked back to Seb.

"Am I not allowed to do the honors?" I pouted.

"Oh, definitely fucking not," Elliot said. I rolled my eyes and turned my attention back to Seb again.

"Yes, baby. Go get him," I said with a defeated huff. They were going to have to realize that I could take care of myself and that I was just as fucked-up and bloodthirsty as they were. But maybe if I conceded to this, they'd let me join Seb as he tortured the guy for answers.

That could be fun.

Seb winked and stood quickly, walking over to the guy with purpose while we all gathered our things, trying not to make a scene in the small village pub. Elliot followed Seb before we did, and I watched as they both held a knife on either side of the dude's torso. They said something too low for me to hear as the rest of us walked past them and out into the cold December night.

It was snowing, and despite the situation we were

currently in, I took a moment to throw my head back and catch a few snowflakes on my tongue.

"Get in the fucking car, Scarlet," Elliot growled, taking hold of my arm and jerking me in the direction of our SUV.

"Easy, big guy, damn," I said, ripping my arm free and crawling into the back seat with Kenna. "I just wanted to…" He cut off my words by slamming the door in my face. "Dick," I said under my breath. He was going to pay for that.

Seb opened the back hatch, and both he and Elliot started to tie the dude up, gagging him and making sure he couldn't get free. Tristan sat up front, and once the other two were done restraining the asshole, Elliot got into the driver's seat.

"I'll sit back here with him to make sure he doesn't try anything funny," Seb said as he crawled in and sat next to him, holding a gun to his face. All the doors shut, we all buckled up, and Kenna peeked over the seat.

"He's pissed himself," she said, holding back laughter. "What did you say to him, Sebby?"

Seb just smiled and shrugged, that murderous little smirk on his lips that I couldn't wait to kiss off later. But first, answers.

CHAPTER twenty nine

SEBASTIAN

I was jumping up and down on the balls of my feet while Elliot and Tristan strung up our little plaything from the ceiling. There was a secret basement under the garage that Elliot's family had put in for a torture room of sorts. Well, was it technically a torture room? No. It was a wine cellar. But it would work just fine for what I needed to use it for.

Kenna had gone straight to the living room, leaving all the dirty work to us. Not that I minded—I wanted all the dirty work. And I wanted my woman to watch as I did it. I could feel the adrenaline running its course through my body, making me jittery. I was like an addict craving his next fix while it was dangling right in front of him, ripe for the picking.

"I'm staying," Scarlet said to Elliot as he tried to pull her up the stairs.

"Fuck's sake," he said, turning his attention on me. "Do not scar her for life," he warned as he pointed a finger in my face.

"She stabbed a guy like twenty times in the chest and then came all over my leg, El. I think she's fine," I told him. Scarlet grabbed his jaw and gave him a kiss before slapping his ass and gesturing for him to leave. Tristan laughed and whispered something in her ear that made her blush before he left as well.

The door shut above us, leaving us down here with just the glow of a utility light on the floor. Her family's little spy was hanging from the ceiling by his hands, keeping him just high enough that he could touch his toes to the floor. I had knocked him out in the car after he wouldn't stop thrashing and causing a scene, so I walked over to him and slapped him a few times.

"Wakey, wakey, eggs and bakey!" I sang and heard Scarlet laugh behind me. It was going to be fun torturing this asshole with her watching. I wondered if she would get wetter the worse I got. I fucking hoped so. Maybe she'd let me fuck her next to his dead body.

He was still gagged, so when he came to, he blinked against the weird lighting and then started flailing and screaming through the cloth in his mouth. I advanced on him, making his eyes go wide with fear and his feet flail on the floor, trying to get away from me.

I grabbed his jaw, getting my face in his. He was an ugly fucker, pockmarked and red-faced. His beady little eyes were filled with terror as he took me in. I slapped his face lightly a few times, watching him flinch.

"I'm going to take this gag out," I told him. "Because I have some questions I want answers to, and you can't quite answer them like this. But," I said with a dramatic pause, turning to look back at Scarlet, who watched with a smile on her face, "but if you make a scene, I will torture and kill you. Savvy?"

He nodded quickly.

"Good boy," I told him as I ripped off the duct tape in one swift yank. He spat the cloth out of his mouth and took deep gulps of air. "What's your name?" I asked him.

He looked over my shoulder at Scarlet and then back at me.

"Don't fucking look at her," I said as I swung the blade in my hand out and across the underside of his bicep. He screamed, and it was fucking music to my ears.

"Gary."

"Was that so hard?" I asked him. "Nice to meet you, Gary. Now, I have a few questions about who you work for. Think your little brain can manage that?"

He gave me a look that I really didn't appreciate, but I chose to ignore it since he nodded swiftly after.

"You work for her family?"

"Yes," he hissed.

"And I'm guessing they sent you here to keep an eye on us?"

"Yes."

"How'd you find us?"

He smiled and rolled his eyes. I tilted my head at the gesture and sliced into his other arm. He cried out and lifted his legs to try and kick me. I backed up and felt Scarlet come up behind me and wrap her arms around my waist. Her breasts pressed into my back and made my dick swell with need.

"He asked you a question," she said. "But if you don't want to answer, you don't have to. I'd actually love to watch him cut you up until you bleed out. That shit turns me on, and it's been a solid twelve hours since I last had any dick. So, go ahead. Test his patience."

"Fuck," I groaned, dropping my head back and soaking up the sensation of her hand cupping and pressing against my hard cock.

"Fucking whore gypsy," he said and spat towards us. I saw fucking red.

"What the fuck did you just call her?" I asked, peeling myself away from her and getting back in his face. I lifted his shirt and made three quick cuts across his stomach. He screamed and jerked, causing the blood to flow more freely over his skin. "You don't get to talk to her like that and live, dickhead."

He was panting as I used my knife to cut all of his clothes away from his body, leaving his boxers. I didn't want to see his disgusting flaccid micropenis, and neither did Scarlet. His pants reeked of piss, and I swallowed against my gag reflex as I threw them to the side. I stood and made circles around his hanging body, humming before bursting out into song.

"I've got a lovely bunch of coconuts," I sang,

dancing around his hanging body while idly flipping my knife in my hand. I made some fast cuts along his back, soaking up his screams like they were my fucking life source. "There they are all standing in a row, *pop, pop, pop!*" I continued singing and slashing. I looked for Scarlet, and she stared at me while her hand moved inside her jeans, her body leaning against the wall.

"Naughty girl," I said, pointing the knife in her direction. "Don't have too much fun without me, princess." She winked, and I went back to my plaything.

"Big ones, tall ones, some as big as your *head*!" I sang, holding the knife to the corner of his mouth. "Give them a twist, a flick of the wrist," I continued, pressing hard enough into his skin to make blood bloom. "Answer my fucking question, cunt. How'd you find us?"

"I followed you, you dumb fuck."

"Your tone is hurtful, Gary," I said, a frown forming on my face. I pressed a bit harder into his mouth, relishing in the sharp intake of breath and his eyes going wider. "But I'll let it slide for now. Why does her family want her?"

His blood was flowing freely from all of his cuts, staining his legs and the floor red. Behind me, I could hear Scarlet's heavy breathing and breathy little moans. This shit needed to end soon. Her pleasure belonged to me, and he was making me miss out on all the fun.

"You may as well just answer me, Gary. I'm sorry to tell you I'm going to kill you anyway. Why not clear that conscience?"

He was silent.

"Gary," I said, my irritation showing through my voice. "You're really testing my patience. Can you pretty please with cherries on top fucking tell me why you're following my fucking woman?"

"Obviously because they want her dead, numb-nuts," he said, a sickly sweet smile on his face. I was not impressed.

"Okay," I said, my face falling flat. "I'm done." Scarlet's hand wrapped around mine, keeping it from slashing across his cheek.

"The boys aren't going to be happy if you don't give him more of an opportunity to answer, babe," she said softly into my ear.

"Can you please just fucking answer so that I can go have sex with my girl?" I begged him in a whiny voice. They were always so stubborn. His eyes moved from me to Scarlet.

"They really want you out of the way, princess," he said, leering at her like she was a piece of meat. "What a fucking disappointment you are, Scarlet," he said. "Such a slut, running around with the enemy, sucking and fucking them like a dime store whore. No wonder your father wants you six feet under, you stupid cunt."

He barely got the last word out before I shoved my blade into his mouth and came away with his tongue.

"That wasn't very nice of you, Gary!" I shouted over his panicked screaming. Scarlet kissed my sweaty neck, her hands working their way down my torso.

"Since he can't talk, Seb," she whispered before nibbling at my flesh. "Just go ahead and kill him." Her fingers worked the button and zipper of my pants, pushing them open and down my thighs. "I want you to fuck me in his blood."

My cock throbbed as her hand wrapped around it through my boxers and then moved to cup my balls in her hot palm.

"Or," she said, dragging her hand back up my length, the tips of her fingers toying with my piercing, "we could make him watch."

I slit his throat instantly, spraying his blood all over both of us. He coughed, and within seconds, his eyes went dark.

"No one gets to see this pussy," I said, turning around and roughly grabbing her through her denim. "No one but us." I held my bloody knife under her chin, the point pressing into her pale skin, making blood well. She smiled and made my cock twitch. My violent girl. "Understood, pet?"

"Understood."

CHAPTER
thirty

SCARLET

The point of his blade was digging into my skin, making a small cut. He pushed it deeper, making me wince, before pulling it away and latching onto the nick with his hot mouth. He sucked, and my head fell back, allowing him full access to my neck.

His lips came away in a bloody smile as he looked at me. The knife dropped to the floor, and his hands seized my face as he kissed me, the iron taste of my blood flooding my mouth. My hands pushed down his boxers as his hands moved from my face to my jeans, shoving them off my hips.

We kicked them off, stripping down to nothing like our lives depended on it as he backed me up against a wall. He lifted me, and I wrapped my legs around his waist. As he shoved himself inside me in one quick thrust, the cool metal of his piercing setting my nerves on fire, my head dropped back against the wall.

I gripped his throat, my nails digging into his flesh, and let him set the pace. He was covered in blood and sweat, his muscles rippling with each thrust inside me, and he had never looked more beautiful to me. His hands gripped my ass, squeezing and spreading me for him.

"Fuck, I love you," he said in a breathy voice as he continued to push me into the wall. I took his mouth in another violent kiss and then rested my forehead against his.

"I love you," I told him. He picked up his pace, hitting that sweet fucking spot inside me over and over again. "Fuck, Seb," I moaned against his lips.

"Come for me, baby."

I whimpered and let go, letting the heat build up in my belly, wrapping around my lower spine.

"Yes, Scarlet," he encouraged. "Let go for me. Let me feel you come apart."

"Shut up," I said, putting my hand over his mouth to concentrate on the feeling spreading through my body. "Right there," I told him over and over again as his hips moved harder against me.

As my orgasm crashed through me, pulsing and squeezing him, he groaned and dropped his head against my shoulder. I felt him come deep inside me, my name coming off his lips like it was our little secret.

Breathing heavily, we stood there, our bodies joined together, kissing and murmuring stupid lovely things to each other for a moment. His mouth moved over every inch of skin he could get to, licking and sucking the beads of sweat from my skin.

"I can't decide what about you tastes the best," he said, making his way back to my mouth. "Your sweat, your blood, your cunt, your fucking mouth." He pressed me tightly against the wall, letting his hands wander up over my hips, my breasts, and then cupping my face as he continued to explore my mouth.

After he had kissed me dizzy, he gently pulled himself out and let me slowly drop back to the floor. One of his hands immediately went in between my legs, shoving two fingers deep inside. I gasped and gripped onto his forearm.

"God, that's hot," he said as his fingers continued exploring. "What a mess we made, little pet." He groaned and slipped his fingers out to circle my clit and then pushed back in. He kept doing that over and over again, demanding that my body give him another orgasm.

"Seb, I— I can't," I told him, trying to hold myself up on weak knees while his talented fingers brought me closer and closer to another wave of electricity.

"Yes, you can," he said, his free hand finding my throat. "And you will."

He squeezed my throat at the same time that he ground his palm against my clit and his fingertips pulsed against my G-spot. I made a noise I wasn't entirely convinced was human, somewhere between a scream and a growl, as my entire body went taut with pleasure. My breathing stopped, and my eyes rolled back as he held my entire body up with his hand at my throat and his fingers in my cunt.

"Good girl," he purred, soaking up every little move my body made. When I came back down, he pulled his fingers free and brought them to his mouth with a cheeky grin. "We taste good together, babe."

I gave him a weak laugh and leaned forward, collapsing into his body.

"Time to bring in the cleanup crew," he said, wrapping his arms around me. "Let's get somewhat put back together and head upstairs. They aren't going to be happy I was too distracted to get all the answers."

"As if they can say they would've done any different," I said, giving him a hard smack on the ass. I pulled my jeans back up, cringing at the wetness leaking down my thighs. "I'm going to shower, and then I'll join you guys," I told him, glancing over at the corpse of Gary limply hanging from the ceiling. I gave him a little shove and watched him swing. I didn't recognize him from anywhere. My family must've gotten new people since I ran away.

"Don't recognize him?" Seb asked as he got dressed.

"I don't," I said. "Not surprising though. I haven't been around for a while." I turned back to Seb. "The cleanup crew stays away from Kenna, got it? Dicks remain in trousers."

He held his hands up in surrender and laughed as I made my way back up the stairs. I wasn't going to have her completely thrown into this life. I wanted to keep her at arm's length, still my best friend but never directly involved with anyone.

I didn't want Kenna to be condemned to a life of worrying when the next attempt on your or your man's life was going to come. It was a stress I grew up with and continued to live with. My body was adjusted; Kenna's wasn't. I wanted to keep her safe, keep her happy. I didn't want to worry about someone using her to get to me.

Kenna looked at me as I stepped into the living room. Her makeup was off, her dark hair pulled up into a messy bun, and she was dressed in baggy sweats. She was so effortlessly pretty with her little upturned nose and dark eyes that seemed to always smile. It was going to be hard to keep the other guys away from her. I was already starting to feel like an overprotective mother hen.

Touch her and die vibes was what I was hoping to give off once they all showed up.

"Guys will be here in a couple hours," Tristan said, looking up at me from his phone.

"I figured they would be. We need the cleanup crew. Seb made a fucking mess."

Tristan's eyes roved over my body with a lingering smile.

"Yeah, he did," he said, winking at me.

Kenna looked at me and made an overexaggerated gagging noise.

"I'm going to shower," I told them, laughing at Kenna.

"And I'm coming with you. Someone needs to wash

your hair," Tristan said. I smiled and backed up slowly, watching as he stood.

"Only if you can catch me," I said and took off up the stairs as he chased after me. I squealed and laughed as we both tumbled up the stairs, fighting to see who would get there first.

I lost.

CHAPTER
thirty one

SCARLET

A couple of hours later, we were all sitting in the living room with Niko and Finn. A couple of other guys were down in the basement, cleaning up the mess Seb had made of Gary.

"Sebastian was too distracted to ask all the questions and get the answers we needed," Elliot said in his normal optimistic tone.

"Enough with the blaming," I told him. "It's hard to focus with this," I said, gesturing to myself, "standing in the room with you."

That earned me a reluctant smile from Elliot and laughs from the other guys. I glanced around and saw Finn staring at Kenna. I cleared my throat, and he looked over at me. With a slow shake of my head, his eyes went a bit wide before he made a show of not looking in her direction anymore.

"All we know is that they want her out of the way," Seb said. "That's all we need to know."

"They don't just want me out of the way," I told them, sticking my cold feet under Tristan's thighs. It was late, after midnight, seeing as how they had to drive here from London, and Kenna was yawning. "They want me dead."

"It would be nice to know why," Elliot mumbled. I shot him the bird.

"The obvious answer is that they want to make sure I won't make any type of claim to their precious throne," I said as I rolled my eyes. "Which…" I trailed off, not wanting to admit what I was about to say. But it was about time I started thinking with a critical mind instead of with whatever I had left of a heart.

"What, poppet?" Tristan asked, leaning over and taking a strand of my hair to play with.

"It could possibly mean that Motshan isn't on my side. Or, at least, that maybe he doesn't know there's a side to pick."

"Not ta be the downer, here," Niko said, chiming in with his Irish accent. I saw Kenna's ears prick up like a damn dog. "I highly doubt your family hasn't informed him there are sides ta pick. But—" He paused. "—that doesn't mean he has all the information. I'm sure they've told him their incredibly biased version," he told me in a reassuring tone.

"My thoughts exactly," Tristan said, running his thumb over my cheek. "That doesn't mean there's no hope for him. It just means we have to get him on our side."

"So we bring him here," I said. "We get a message to him and bring him here. Niko?" I asked, looking to him for support.

"Oh, hell no," Elliot chimed in first. "That is a disaster waiting to fucking happen. You tell him to meet you here, he brings the fucking army with him. No chance in hell."

"Why does that even matter at this point? Gary has been here for how long, and you really don't think he had already reported back where we were? Don't be daft," I scoffed. "If they wanted to get here, they could."

"She's got a point," Finn said, still making obvious efforts to not look at Kenna. She seemed to find it funny, scooting closer to him and doing little things to try and get his eyes back on her. "If they wanted to ambush, they'd ambush."

"And it might be smarter to get ahead of it," Seb said, leaning forward so that he could see everyone. "They're going to realize pretty quickly that something is wrong when dear old Gary doesn't check in. They may already be suspicious. They won't have heard from him in hours."

"Good point," Niko said. "Want me to give Simon a ring? Get him to start working on this?"

"Thank you, Niko," I said to him as he got the nod from Tristan and stood to make his call outside.

"You're still putting her directly in the line of fire," Elliot said.

"If you're so concerned about her well-being in this situation, Man Bun," Kenna jumped in, "then you be the one to protect her. Don't leave her side, and make sure she's okay. Stop fighting something that is clearly going to happen, and just make sure it doesn't go *wrong*."

"What Kenneth said," Seb agreed. Kenna leaned up and smacked him upside the head. "Ouch, K-Dawg! Not nice," he admonished with a smile, rubbing the back of his head.

"Kenna," I said, grabbing her attention. "Do you want to go home? You don't need to be here for this. This isn't your world, and it definitely isn't your fight." What I really wanted to do was ship her back to London whether she liked it or not, but I wasn't going to treat her like a child or like she was somehow weaker than me. I didn't want her to feel like I was taking her choice away.

"I can take her," Finn said at the same time that Tristan shut it down.

"She needs to stay here," he said.

"I don't want to leave anyway. I feel safer here with you guys than I would feel at home…you know…without a door," she said.

"I fixed that for you," Finn said. "You have a door that works again. I went over that night and did it."

"Thanks," she said with a little smile, her cheeks reddening.

Fuck my life, I thought to myself. *She would want to get into someone's pants.*

"Are you sure?" I asked her, pulling her attention

back to me. "Ignore Tristan. If you really want to leave, we can get you to a different safe house. They can spare a few men to stay with you until everything settles down."

"I'd be happy—" I cut Finn off by holding up my hand in his direction before he could finish his sentence.

"Honestly," she said, looking at me earnestly. "I'd prefer to stay here."

"Okay," I conceded. "But I'm going to be clucking around you like a mother hen." I turned my attention to my three guys, making sure to look each one of them in the eyes as I said it. "She is protected at all times, yeah?"

They all agreed.

"I'm serious. I want guys with eyes on her all the time. Someone needs to stay with her."

"It's not going to be us," Elliot said. I looked over at him, shocked at what he was saying. I opened my mouth to tell him off, but he held his hand up. "Before you flip your shit, little one. All three of us are going to be distracted and worried about *you*."

"True," Seb agreed. "We won't be the best people for it. I'll be too distracted by how your ass looks in whatever jeans you wear as you go on a killing spree."

"I'm not going on a killing spree," I told him.

"Let Finn take care of her," Tristan announced with a knowing smile.

"That works!" Kenna perked up before I could shut it down. I looked at Tristan to find him smiling at me like he knew what he'd done. I narrowed my eyes at him and then looked over at Finn.

"Your dick stays in your pants, or I cut it off, yeah?" I asked him.

Seb snorted.

"Yes, ma'am," Finn said, his cheeks turning a bright red that almost made him more attractive. Gingers had never been my thing, but he had the whole lumberjack look going for him. I guessed Kenna could do worse.

"Good. I'm going to bed. I have a feeling the next few days are going to be long."

"My turn," Elliot said, standing up and quickly grabbing me to throw me over his shoulder. He turned around to let Tristan and Seb give me a kiss before carrying me up the stairs.

Now all we had to do was wait and hope Motshan would pull through.

CHAPTER
thirty two

SCARLET

The next few days passed in a blur. Men were coming and going every few hours to touch base and have little meetings that were so boring I ended up skipping out on them and watching more trash TV with Kenna. Niko had gone back to London to help keep shit under control there with Simon. But Finn was hanging around with us, keeping Kenna entertained when I had to be with the boys, and trying to get on my good side when we all hung out together.

"Are you sure the neighbors aren't going to call the cops?" Kenna asked for the third time in the last twenty-four hours. "You guys literally look like you're running a drug ring out of this small suburban home."

"It isn't small," Seb mumbled.

"Even if they did," I told her, giving Seb a look that

told him not to fucking start, "these assholes have their fingers in every pie. It would be fine."

"Got our fingers in *your* pie." Seb laughed to himself. I rolled my eyes and ignored him.

"Alright," Tristan said as he walked into the living room. "Motshan got back to Simon. It's a go. He'll be here tonight at five."

"Oh, great," Elliot said. "Right as it gets dark. Wonder why that is." His tone was weighed down with sarcasm.

"A little optimistic thinking, please, Elliot," I begged. He had turned into his usual sour self the past few days with all the men, the planning, and, of course, the whole meeting with Motshan that he didn't agree with. He was fighting with me hourly about how stupid my decisions were. I knew that his worries came from a good place, but if he didn't chill the fuck out, I was going to take out my frustrations on him in a way he wouldn't enjoy.

"So, we have, what?" Kenna asked, looking up at the clock on the wall. "Two hours to prepare for this?"

"Two hours," I agreed, looking around at everyone. "Let's do this."

"He isn't going to want any of you in here," I told all three of my guys. We were standing in the living room, anxiously looking through the curtains, waiting for the headlights we were all expecting. "He's going to want me alone."

"I really don't like this," Elliot said again. "I have a really bad fucking feeling."

"You always have a bad feeling, big guy," I joked, nudging his side with my body. "Honestly, there's nothing else we can really do at this point," I told him. "I can't stay here forever. You guys can't stay here forever. At some point this shit needs to be settled. And I really think Motshan can be the missing link to all of that. If he's anything like he used to be, or if he will at least hear me out…this could be the way to finish this and get back to our lives."

Tristan leaned over and kissed my hair.

"We aren't going to leave you completely alone," he said. "You guys can have the room to yourselves, but we aren't leaving the house. Our men will be outside, making rounds around the house, and we'll be inside but just out of earshot to give you guys privacy. If you yell though, we'll hear you."

"And Finn will be upstairs in my bedroom with Kenna," Seb said. "It's the one that's set back the furthest. Makes sense to keep her as far away from it all as possible."

"Headlights," Finn said from the window.

"Showtime," I said, my stomach suddenly swirling with nerves. I hadn't seen him in so long. I was terrified and excited all at once. I wanted him to be the same boy I knew all those years ago: friendly, kind, and funny. But the boys had gotten into my head. Maybe they had taken him away from me to train him, groom him, and turn him into my dad. I shivered at the thought.

"Good luck, babe," Kenna said, kissing my cheek.

She walked upstairs with Finn, leaving just me, Tristan, Seb, and Elliot in the living room. There were about ten guys outside, walking around the house and the neighborhood, always on the lookout for any type of ambush.

I walked over to the window and watched the sleek car pull into the driveway. Motshan stepped out and looked around, pushing a hand through his neatly styled hair. The sun was almost completely set, and as he looked up at the window, we locked eyes, and he lifted his hand in a wave.

I waved back and let the curtain fall.

"Alright, you guys go away. Let me get this shit over with."

"I will literally disembowel him if he so much as lays a finger on you with any sort of attitude," Seb said. I gave him a salute and let them each give me a kiss before making my way over to the door.

My heart was trying to make its way out of my chest. I wanted this to go well. I *needed* it to go well. He knocked on the door and took a deep breath, trying to control my racing heart. I was torn between wanting to throw myself on him for a hug and playing it cool, not letting him see me with my emotions on display. I didn't know what to expect with him, and it was throwing me off my game.

I finally twisted the knob and opened the door. God, he had gotten older. And taller. His black hair was slicked back, accentuating cheekbones that could cut glass. His eyes were still my eyes, crystal clear and blue.

But there was something about him that screamed maturity now, no longer a little boy running through the halls playing hide-and-seek with his cousin.

"Scarlet," he said with a smile. He opened his arms, welcoming me in for a hug. I could've cried with relief.

"Motshan," I breathed, walking into his arms and wrapping mine around him. "You're so tall!" I told him.

"And you're not," he said, his Romanian accent giving his voice a certain lilt. He laughed and mussed my hair before walking the rest of the way in the house. He looked around, taking in his surroundings before gesturing towards the living room, asking if that was where we were going.

"Yeah, yeah," I said, closing the front door and leading him inside. "I don't even know where to start," I admitted, sitting on the couch across from him. "How have you been? *Where* have you been? How did they get you back here?"

"Well, I've been stuck in Romania with the family until a few weeks ago. They randomly brought me back —well, your dad did. I guess I'm here to run this stupid business once he decides to retire or kick the bucket." He settled back into the couch and crossed an ankle on a knee. "Unless you want it…"

CHAPTER
thirty three

SCARLET

I stared at him for a moment. That definitely wasn't what I thought was going to come out of his mouth. Was he testing me?

"I don't want it, Motshan," I told him with as stern a voice as I could muster in the moment. "Why the fuck would I want to run a family that tried to have me killed? You are more than welcome to their fucked-up little throne."

"What do you mean they tried to have you killed?" he asked, his face filled with shock.

"On my twenty-first birthday, I went to sleep and woke up with someone on top of me trying to kill me. It had to be them. I was screaming until my lungs hurt and no one came. And you know as well as I do, that fucking house was never left unattended."

"Jesus Christ," he said, leaning up and running his hands over his face. "This is so much more fucked-up than I thought it was. Not that I expected them to tell me the full truth," he continued. "But they told me you—and I quote—abandoned the family for cock."

"They would say something like that. Father always did have a way with words." I sighed and made sure Motshan was looking at me before I continued. "They're liars, Motshan. It's what they do. I didn't abandon the family, Motshan," I told him sincerely. "I didn't have any plans to. I mean, what would I have even done with my life? No. I only ran away because it was that or be killed. I lived on the streets for a while before I found odd jobs and shitty roommates to take me in.

"It wasn't until I met my friend Kenna that I actually got back on my feet. She gave me a place to stay and helped me find jobs that paid better. And I didn't meet these assholes until they came to a house party to kidnap me for ransom." I smiled and rolled my eyes at the memory.

"But you are fucking them?" he asked. When I opened my mouth to put him in his place, he laughed. "I'm not judging you, cousin. I mean, who could say no? Especially blondie?" He made a show of fanning himself and leaned back on the couch.

I laughed hysterically.

"Oh my god, Motshan. Does Dad know you're…?" I trailed off and raised my eyebrows at him, giving him a look.

"What? Into the person regardless of the equipment?" he deadpanned. I nodded, holding back more laughter, because this really wasn't a light-hearted conversation in a family like ours. It wasn't allowed. It wasn't discussed. And you sure as shit didn't choose a replacement that wouldn't be spilling seed for an heir.

"Not something I go around broadcasting," he said. "Anyway," he said, abruptly changing the subject, "do I get to meet your boyfriends?"

"If you want." I smiled. "They agreed to let me handle this alone if I wanted."

"So they treat you well?"

I thought back to my time with them, my brain snagging on the time I spent with Elliot in the garage. Not that I could fault him for trying to take care of his family. He wouldn't be the man I fell for if he hadn't. But there had been so many times they offered me my independence when I wanted it. They treated me better than any other relationship I had ever been in, despite being the leaders of a top crime syndicate.

"They do. And before I bring them in here, I'd really like to talk about what this means for us, for our future. Because if you're back, and you're on my side in all of this, it would really take some serious shit off my shoulders," I told him.

"Scarlet, I've always been on your side, you know that. But I'm waiting in the wings. I don't have any sort of pull yet, especially when it comes to something like this. I don't speak for the family, and I definitely don't speak for your father." He sighed and leaned forward again, his face turning serious. "I can't offer you what you want."

"What do you think I want?" I asked him.

"You want me to tell you that I can stop this stupid little tiff between our family and your Triad," I stated.

"It isn't *my* Triad," I insisted.

"Your pussy is wetting their dicks," he said with a laugh. "It's as yours as it ever can be. They're letting you take meetings by yourself. They killed a lot of people to rescue you. They kept you safe from your dad. They're yours, which in turn means their gang is yours."

"Okay," I said, choosing to leave that fight for another day. That wasn't what I had asked him to meet me for. "Where do we go from here, then?" I asked. "I would really like to get Dad to leave me the fuck alone. I don't want his legacy. I don't want or need his money. I don't want or need any communication with him ever again. He can forget I was ever born if he wants. I just need him to leave me and the boys alone."

"And to stay on his own turf," Motshan interjected.

"Yeah, that too," I sighed. "This shit isn't going to stop unless we can call a ceasefire."

"I told you, I don't have that kind of sway."

"Motshan," I said, my annoyance beginning to leak into my tone. "I understand you don't have that sway yet. But you aren't useless. He's grooming you to take his place, which means he *will* listen to you. You have his ear, which is something I will never have. Will you please help me out here?"

He looked down at his hands folded between his legs, and I followed his gaze, noticing for the first time his scarred skin and bruised knuckles. My gaze wandered up his body, taking in all the little scars here and there that weren't as noticeable at first. His entire face had old nicks and cuts that continued down his neck. What the fuck had he been through?

"Of course I can," he finally said. "The only reason I'm hesitant to say this is because I don't want to get your hopes up." He paused for a moment, and I stayed quiet, letting him gather his thoughts. I didn't want to push him too hard and end up pushing him away.

"You know how he is," he eventually said. "I have to balance this shit. I can't go in guns blazing because he's going to think I've turned, that I'm weak. If you want me to take over and be your ally in the long run, we have to be careful how we play this. It isn't going to be an immediate change. He isn't going to just give up."

"That makes sense," Tristan said from the doorway. I jumped at his voice and turned to see all three of them standing there. "Tristan," he said, introducing himself and extending his hand as he walked over to Motshan.

"Motshan," he answered, shaking his hand. They went down the line, getting pleasantries out of the way before they all sat down in the living room with us. Seb sat so close to me he might as well have been on top of me, placing a possessive hand on my thigh. Motshan's eye caught it, and he smiled.

"We agreed to let Scarlet handle this," Tristan said, taking on his role as leader in front of the outsider. "But I felt you needed to meet us, put faces to the names, and realize we aren't a threat to you." Tristan paused, looking over at me quickly before his eyes moved back to Motshan. "We love your cousin," he said, and I felt my pulse jump. "We want this to end so that she can finally have a life that's not filled with looking over her shoulder every five minutes."

Motshan said something back, but I was too busy staring at Tristan, my eyes wide and my blood rushing loudly through my ears. I'd never had the love of one man, let alone two. I hadn't even heard my father ever say those words to me.

I finally realized Motshan was trying to get my attention.

"Yeah?" I asked, blinking back to the moment.

"I need to head out," he said, standing. "I'll talk to him and be in touch, okay?"

I stood and squeezed him, missing the little boy I used to know but choosing to trust the man in front of me.

"Just get with Simon for anything, yeah?" I asked him, walking him towards the door. "He will let all of us know, and we can meet up again or something."

"Of course," he said, pausing at the doorway and shaking the guys' hands again. "Good to meet you guys. We'll talk more later." He checked his watch. "Take care of her, yeah?" he said, looking at each of them.

Then he looked at me, grabbing the back of my neck and pulling me in to kiss my forehead.

"I'm sorry," he whispered and then opened the door and backed out.

"What?" I asked, confused, before looking around

and seeing all of our men scattered around the front yard, either dead or completely knocked out. I couldn't tell under the cover of darkness. "What…?" I whispered.

Elliot grabbed my arm, pushing me behind all three of them as headlights flooded the road, and my father stepped out of Motshan's car.

CHAPTER
thirty four

SCARLET

I fought through my boys, pushing in between them so that I could get a good look at the father who had tried to have me killed. More men filed out of the few cars that had pulled up. With all of our men out cold on the ground, we were outnumbered at least three to one.

"Not to say I told you so, but…" Elliot said.

"Shut the fuck up, Elliot," Seb said.

Tristan pushed past all of us and walked out of the doorway.

"Can we help you?" he asked my father.

"Hello, Scarlet," my father said, staying close to the car.

"Father," I said flatly. Motshan made his way next to my father, his hands clasped behind his back. "How disappointing," I said, locking eyes with Motshan. He had a blank look on his face, but a sad smile tugged at his lips.

"I'm sad to have missed the reunion," my father exclaimed, clapping his hands together. "But it's nice to see you both all grown up! You both look so similar!" he said with a smile, grabbing Motshan's cheek and giving it a squeeze. "Romani blood runs strong in this family!"

Motshan pulled his face free and took a step away, creating some distance between them.

"Not that I should expect anything less from my own children."

I took a step forward, blood rushing through my head again, making me dizzy. Somewhere behind me, I heard Finn come down the stairs and take in the scene. They all began to murmur and whisper, talking about me quite literally behind my back. I felt the blood rush to my face. How could I have been so fucking stupid?

"What are you saying?" I asked him as I took a few steps forward. I felt the guys follow close behind as the ten or so men my father had tensed. Motshan's face was a grimace, staring in my direction but just past me, refusing to make eye contact. "What are you saying!" I shouted, my temper boiling over.

"Oh, he didn't tell you?" my father asked with a sick smile on his face. "He's your brother! Next in line to run this family," he said as he clapped Motshan on the back. "And this was his final test, wasn't it, son?"

"What was?" I asked, advancing on them a few more steps. Every single man standing around suddenly had their hands on their weapons, tensing and taking a step a bit closer to my dad. He was surrounded by his men, guns aimed at me and my boys behind me.

"Getting us to you, little girl," he answered.

"You're a liar," I told him. "You're all fucking liars. You've lied to me since I was old enough to understand the word. You told me that he was my cousin. You *took* him from me. You tried to have me killed. And you've done nothing but lie to him since he came back, haven't you?"

My anger was its own entity, hot and rabid, rolling through my body like a storm. I felt my entire body flush with it, every muscle in my body straining with the effort to not claw his eyes out of his fucking sockets.

"So dramatic," my father said, rolling his eyes. "You were always such a brat."

"Fuck you," I spat, my fury getting the best of me. I grabbed my Glock out of the back of my waistband and began shooting. I heard gunfire going off all around me, but my priority was getting to him. Getting to him to kill him for fucking with my life, lying to me and Motshan, and pitting him against me. He deserved to die, and it deserved to be by my fucking hand.

I aimed and shot at everyone around him, my boys behind me taking out the men who tried to get to me first. I counted the rounds as they popped out of my gun, hitting men on his left and right. His men fell in heaps at his feet, like useless sacks of potatoes.

I stopped at thirteen shots fired, my lucky number. I had two shots left.

"Scarlet!" I heard Elliot yell from behind me as I

ran up to my father and pushed my gun into his temple.

"This was always so stupid of you," I spat in his reddened face. His eyes had gone wide with fear. "Relying on others to keep you safe, never carrying a gun yourself and letting others take the fucking fall." I gripped his shirt and moved my gun, shoving it into his mouth as I pushed him down onto his knees.

"I have two bullets left, Father," I told him, watching with glee as sweat poured down his forehead. "One to make you feel pain," I said, pulling the gun out and shooting him in his right shoulder. He screamed, and I took the opportunity of his open mouth to shove the barrel of my gun back in.

"And one to kill you."

"Not happening, Scarlet," Motshan said from behind me, pressing his gun to the back of my head. I didn't even care; I just pushed mine further into my father's mouth, forcing it into his throat as his shoulder bled and tears streamed down his face. He looked pathetic on his knees beneath me.

I fucking loved it.

"Don't do it, Scarlet," Motshan said in his stupid fucking Romanian lilt that I had found so charming not even an hour ago. I felt my throat close and tears threaten to fall. "I *will* fucking shoot you. Please, don't make me do it, Scarlet."

"You are a piece of trash," I said down to my father as I felt my lip curl and heat crash through my body. "You lived a selfish, pathetic little life."

"Scarlet!" I heard Kenna scream from behind me.

Time slowed down as I felt Motshan turn, his gun abandoning the back of my head. I turned around, following the aim of his gun as it moved towards Kenna.

"No!" I shouted. Suddenly there was Finn, shoving Kenna out of the way and jumping into the line of fire. The crack of Motshan's gun sounded through my brain, ricocheting, sending bolts of panic through every nerve in my body.

The bullet connected, sending Finn backwards, blood spraying all over Kenna. His face twisted in pain, and I took off, running to stop the bleeding as his body collided with the concrete.

"Not so fast," my father said, grabbing my arm and gripping it until I knew bruises would form. I swung around, aiming mine directly between his eyes.

"Put it down," Motshan said, his gun somehow aimed back at me, pointing directly at my forehead. "No one helps him!" Motshan yelled. "Not until Scarlet puts down her fucking gun!"

"Motshan," I pleaded. "Don't do this, please." I looked down at Finn, his helpless body bleeding and unconscious on the ground. Tristan, Elliot, and Sebastian were all standing closest to him and Kenna, looking between Motshan and Finn, trying to gauge if they could make it to him.

"If you think I won't kill her," Motshan said, connecting his gun to my cheek, "you are sorely mistaken. Tell her to put her fucking gun down, and I'll let you help him."

No one spoke. No one moved. They were letting

me choose. They knew how important the moment was for me. My boys were going to let me make the decision.

"Scarlet," Kenna said, her voice betraying her emotion. I moved my gaze to her, and even in the dark, I could see her emotions written all over her face.

I sighed and squatted down slowly, setting my gun down on the concrete.

"Good girl," my father said, and a chill worked its way up my spine. Motshan's arm came around my shoulders, pulling me into his side as Tristan and Kenna went to Finn, fisting the wound on his chest.

"You know what?" Motshan asked, drawing everyone's attention. "I think we'll just take my sister with us," Motshan said. "For safekeeping."

CHAPTER
thirty five

SEBASTIAN

My gun was empty, and they were going to take my girl from me again.

I saw black. I saw red. I saw every fucking color of the goddamn rainbow at the thought of losing her again. Tristan was frozen, his phone to his ear as he called paramedics for Finn, who was quickly losing all of his color. Kenna was crying, holding Finn's head in her lap. Elliot was frozen, staring at the scene before him like he had never seen death before.

I would die before I let them take her away from me. I had lost Mel. I thought I had lost Scarlet only a few weeks ago. I couldn't go through that again. I would lose my sanity.

"Over my dead body!" I shouted at him as I grabbed Elliot's gun out of his hand and charged towards them.

Motshan aimed his gun directly at me and shot. The pain was instant but not enough to stop the adrenaline flooding my system. I had to get Scarlet out of that fucking car.

I heard Scarlet's terrified scream as I kept going, raising my own gun directly at her father, and shot. I watched as the bullet fired and hit its mark, sending her father backwards, brain matter exploding all over the drive.

"Fuck's sake!" Motshan yelled, shooting me again, this time in my stomach. I went down on my knees, my body unable to stand against the pain anymore. He shoved Scarlet away from him and worked quickly to get their father's fat ass in the back seat instead.

Scarlet crawled over to me in a panic, her voice hoarse and tears cascading down her face as she leaned over me. My vision was going in and out. I saw Motshan take one last look at her over my body before he got in the car, slamming the door and driving away.

The front yard was littered with dead bodies, and I suddenly thought I might be one of them. My hand came away from my stomach coated in blood. I held it up in front of my face, shocked that a person could bleed that much so quickly.

Scarlet's eyes went wide as she took in my wounds, the bad one in my stomach and the other in my left arm. My body started going cold as Scarlet screamed for Elliot and Tristan.

"Tell them to hurry!" she screamed at Tristan. Elliot ran over, his legs suddenly seeming to work again, and fell to his knees next to me.

"Not going to happen, brother," Elliot said, pressing his hands painfully onto my stomach. "You are not dying today, okay? She'll be impossible," he said, nodding towards Scarlet. I laughed and then coughed as the taste of blood spilled into my mouth. I turned my head and spat it out.

"No, no, no, baby," Scarlet said, her voice thick with tears. "You don't get to leave me, okay? Don't leave me with the asshole and the pretty boy. I won't be able to take it." She tried to smile but failed as she choked on a sob.

She was beautiful when she cried, her mascara and eyeliner painting her cheeks black with war paint. I had never been more proud of her than I had been watching her shoot her father. I was sad she didn't get to be the one to kill him, but there was no stopping me when I thought they were going to take her.

I'd let her kill her brother to make up for it. That would be a good Christmas present.

I coughed again, and more blood spilled into my mouth.

If I survived to see Christmas, I guessed.

"Tristan!" Scarlet shouted again, her voice shrill with panic.

"They're on their way, Scarlet!" he shouted back. I heard him murmur something to Kenna and then his footsteps as he ran over to me.

"How's Finn?" I asked, trying to steady my heart against the pain and panic. I needed to get myself under control so that I didn't make the bleeding worse.

Elliot pushed harder on my stomach, and I cried out at the sharp pain that flooded my system.

"I'm sorry," he said, sounding incredibly genuine for Elliot. Scarlet took my hand and squeezed before leaning over me to plant kisses on my forehead and push my hair out of my face. It was getting so long, I thought to myself. I'd have to get it cut if I survived the night.

"The medics just need to get here," Tristan answered.

"Hey!" Scarlet said, slapping my face. "Don't fall asleep."

Had I?

I looked around, taking in all of their worried faces. My body was very, very cold. All I wanted to do was sleep. A few minutes of peace couldn't hurt.

Scarlet's warm mouth covered mine. Her taste was much better than my own blood.

"They're here!" Scarlet cried as blue and red lights began to flash behind her. But all I could think about was taking a fucking nap. I thought I deserved it after being shot…twice. My eyes blinked shut.

"No!" Scarlet said, slapping my face again.

But I didn't care. I was tired, and my body was numb. I just wanted five minutes.

"No, no, no!" I heard Scarlet cry as someone began pumping my chest in a steady rhythm, lulling me into the blackness.

EPILOGUE

MOTSHAN

"What the *fuck* am I going to do now?" I yelled into the car. "Fuck, fuck, fuck!"

I drove down the road, dear old dad dead in the back seat. I needed to come up with a story and fast. I hadn't planned for him to die yet. That was supposed to be saved for Scarlet, a payback for all the shit he put us through as kids.

Shipping me off to Romania was just the start of it for me. He sent me there, putting me into the *care* of the old family. It had been brutal from day one. I was treated worse than a dog, shoved into fight after fight, even as a child. My entire body was covered in scars from the shit they had put me through.

They had tried to turn me against Scarlet every day, telling me how it was her fault I was sent there and how she had wanted me gone. They didn't expect me to be smart enough, even as a ten-year-old, to know what they were doing.

"Think!" I yelled at myself, smacking my hand against the steering wheel as I sped back to London. There was no getting around that I was going to have to place the blame for this on the Triad. There was no getting Scarlet and her men out of this unscathed, no matter how badly I wanted this stupidity to end.

Sebastian had taken it out of my hands, starting a war I would be helpless against stopping.

ACKNOWLEDGMENTS

Firstly, I want to thank the readers. This book is dedicated to you because this started it all. I was able to quit my job and write full time all because of you and your endless love and support. I can't imagine where I would be without you all. Thank you so, so much.

A special thanks to all of my friends who kept me on track through this one. I had a lot of doubts when it came to Liars. I was fighting through some hard core imposter syndrome and I had never written a book focused *so* much on relationship building and not so much the other stuff. You guys kept me sane and made me realize I need to stop fighting where my characters want to go.

Thank you to Abi at Pink Elephant Designs for another amazing cover and formatting. Thank you for working with me as I was running behind and giving me some wiggle room.

Same to you, Sandra at One Love Editing. I seriously don't know how you put up with my constant mania lately. But here we are, continually throwing more wood on the fire. Thank you for always loving what I send you, and making my books the best they can be.

To my PA, Jordin. Girl, I cannot tell you how much you've help me these last months. You have taken so much stress off of my shoulders, I cannot thank you enough. You and Lou have been my rocks. Lou, thanks for yelling at me to put my phone away. (Even though it doesn't always work.)

I'd also like to thank my family. For all of you who knew I was trying to keep this a secret….well….secret's out. They know guys. But, it's okay. I think I've convinced them not to read them, and they were extremely supportive. So huge thanks to my mom and everyone else in the family that now knows for encouraging me to follow my dreams.

See you guys next time!

ABOUT
the author

Dana Isaly is a writer of dark romance, fantasy romance, and has also been known to dabble in poetry (it was a phase in college, leave her alone).

She was born in the Midwest and has been all over but now resides (begrudgingly) in Alabama. She is a lover of books, coffee, and rainy days. Dana is probably the only person in the writing community that is actually a morning person.

She swears too much, is way too comfortable on her TikTok (@authordanaisaly and @auth.danaisaly), and believes that love is love is love.

You can find her on Instagram (@danaisalyauthorpage) or on Facebook with the same name, but she won't lie, Facebook is not her forte.

ALSO BY
Dana Isaly

The Triad Series

Scars (Book 1)

Liars (Book 2)

Book 3

The Esteria Series

Flame and Starlight

Book 2

One Night Series

Games We Play

Secrets We Hunt

Into The Dark

Made in the USA
Columbia, SC
16 July 2024